Lost and Found

Lost and Found

Peggy Weeks

First published in Great Britain in 2017 by

Bannister Publications Ltd
118 Saltergate
Chesterfield
Derbyshire S40 1NG

ISBN 978-1-909813-32-8

Copyright © Peggy Anne Weeks

Peggy Anne Weeks asserts the moral right to be identified
as the author of this work

A catalogue record for this book is available from the British Library

This book is sold subject to the condition that it shall not, by way of trade or otherwise, be lent, re-sold, hired out or otherwise circulated without the copyright holder's prior consent in any form of binding or cover other than that in which it is published and without a similar condition including this condition being imposed on the subsequent purchase.

All rights reserved. No part of this book may be reproduced or transmitted in any form or by any means, electronic or mechanical including photocopying, recording or by any information storage and retrieval system, without permission from the copyright holder, in writing.

All characters in this publication are fictitious and any resemblance to real persons, living or dead is purely coincidental.

Typeset by Escritor Design, Bournemouth

Printed and bound in Great Britain

For my dear friend Iris

Chapter 1

As Fay walked into the dining room she thought how quiet and tranquil it seemed, even more disturbing, she smiled wryly. What had she expected, her life was in tatters and the previous night's events were still clinging to her brain like stale cigar smoke. It was hardly surprising the atmosphere seemed strange and out of kilter.

Suddenly she could hear Thomas's voice.

He had lied to the end, trying every trick and excuse he could think of. As the reality of her situation finally became clear, she had felt sick and stupid. How could I have fallen for his lies. Finally she was seeing the real Thomas. A liar, a cheat even now unable to admit that he was in any way to responsible for the situation they were in.

'Did he have fun turning my life inside out?' she asked herself, 'knowing all the time he wasn't free and had no right to ask me to marry him'. He had a child which somehow made things even worse.

'How could I have been so gullible?' As this thought took hold, Fay felt her eyes sting. She blinked, refusing to let the tears fall, unable to stop her mind racing, trying to keep pace with her emotions, knowing if she gave in she would be lost in her misery, and Thomas wasn't worth shedding tears over.

'Stop and think', she whispered. 'Try to function and work out what to do'. Fragments of last night's conversation kept creeping into her mind. They were all jumbled together, along with the hurt she was feeling, nothing seemed to make sense. Feeling again the awful numbness that seemed to consume her since last night, she could hear Thomas shouting, his voice seemed so loud in her head. It was a nightmare, a dream, surely last night had not really happened?

For a brief moment she tried to convince herself it was some kind of misunderstanding. She couldn't believe how easily she had been taken in.

Fay shook herself and tried to get control of her thoughts. 'Of course it happened and she had to make it right; somehow she had to make it right.'

She turned quickly, leaving the dining room and walked across the hall into the kitchen. Catching sight of her reflection in the window, she sighed, 'I look so pale.' Turning away as her expression changed to a look of quiet determination. ' I need to clear away all tangible evidence of last night.' Picking up a roll of dustbin liners she went back to the dining room.

The table was still set for the romantic dinner she had lovingly cooked for Thomas. Now the food was cold, congealed and looked disgusting. 'Just how I feel,' she thought. Taking hold of a dustbin liner she frantically started pushing everything on the table into the bag. Somewhere in her mind, registering the crash and tinkle of glass, crockery and cutlery colliding. She didn't care, in fact the noise of the destruction was somehow satisfying.

When the table was empty, she stopped and looked around the room for anything else that needed clearing away. Lifting the bag, she carried it through to the kitchen and pushed it into the pedal bin.

Some of the contents spilled out onto the tiled floor, she ignored the mess it made; what did it matter? Then tears which had been held back for so long finally started to fall. She slid to the floor and leant against the wall with her head resting on her arms, draped across pedal bin, oblivious to the sticky mess clinging to her clothes.

As the tears subsided, Fay looked at the broken crockery and spilt food surrounding her.

This mess is not the only thing I have to get rid of, she thought, I have to clear Thomas out of my life. The house is full of him and his broken promises, his lies that had so convinced her of his love. A new start, new job, new home, somewhere away from this town and its memories is what I need. Thomas was no longer a part of her life she had no reason to stay. Getting to her feet Fay headed out of the kitchen and ran up the stairs to start organising her new life. As she made her plans she made a silent vow. 'No man will ever get close enough to wreck my life again. I will never trust any man again.'

Fay smiled as she looked out over the marina. Gibraltar had become her home now, and after three years she had settled well and found her own little niche here. At first it felt as if she was on holiday, then gradually she found the island was in some ways similar to England, and she felt less of a stranger. It took time for her to make friends, and at first she had been lonely, but not once had she regretted her decision to leave England.

When Fay compared her life here to the life she had left behind she felt little sadness. Her upbringing had been unusual; although she had been loved, in the end she was left alone and vulnerable. It hadn't taken long for someone to turn her vulnerability to their advantage.

She learnt the hard way that people were not always what they seemed and couldn't be taken at face value. As time moved on she found the mix of cultures in Gibraltar suited her very well, although she still kept her guard up where friendships were concerned.

There was a good social life on Gibraltar; people here didn't ask too much about other people's backgrounds. Sometimes she thought it was because they had their own skeletons to hide or perhaps a past they wanted to forget. This suited her perfectly, here she could learn to live again and let the pain of the past go.

Fay was employed as a personal assistant by novelist Emma Woodberry. Although she hadn't heard of Emma Woodberry prior to applying for employment, Fay soon discovered she was a very successful author. Working for Emma proved to be the perfect job, although challenging, it was very interesting, added to which a deep friendship had formed between them. Emma was the one person Fay did trust.

When she had first arrived, Emma had helped her to integrate into the 'ex pat' society, introducing her to people and treating her more as friend than an employee. Fay often thanked her lucky stars for having found such a great employer. Emma had never tried to find out why she had left England, she just accepted the answer given at her interview. 'I need a new challenge in my life', Fay had said, 'and Gibraltar seemed as good a place as any to look for it'.

Fay knew instinctively that Emma did not believe this was the reason for her changing her life but she never questioned her about it. She was grateful to her employer for that, as their friendship grew it didn't matter anyway.

Today though, it was different, her employer was unusually tense. Anthony, her son was arriving with his fiancé Leona. Emma had not met her and was hoping that they would like each other. She had no wish to become a wicked mother-in-law. Her own marriage had been blissfully happy until her husband's death.

Emma wanted Anthony to have the same happiness in his life. He was her only son and his well-being was the most important thing to her. His fiancée would have to be a very special lady to impress Emma.

A dinner had been arranged by Emma to welcome them. It would be a glitzy affair held at the casino, neutral ground so to speak. Hopefully then everyone would be more at ease. Perhaps they could gamble a little, or just sit back and enjoy the excellent band; maybe enjoy the occasional dance. It would give them all time to get to know each other without Leona being under any pressure. Fay knew that with the wedding plans already in progress, Emma wanted Leona to feel relaxed and comfortable in Gibraltar.

Fay was looking forward to the evening. Even though she didn't gamble very often, she did enjoy dancing. She didn't have a boyfriend as such but was never without partners at dances she attended. There were several male friends whose company she enjoyed and were always willing to act as her escort. It was rare for her to be without a partner; but tonight was different, she was invited as part of Emma's family group, so would not be taking a partner.

Fay's thoughts were interrupted as she heard footsteps coming towards her office. Emma walked past the open door calling out to Fay.

"Don't forget drinks at the hotel about 8pm, I want you to meet Anthony and Leona before they are lost in the crowd. Anthony has been away so long everyone will want to talk to him."

The door office banged as Emma rushed out, heading home to get herself ready for the evening and not hearing Fay's words of goodbye. Fay smiled to herself. In a hurry as usual! One day I will find out where all her energy comes from.

Looking out of the office window she watched her employer bound down the steps to her car. It must be wonderful to have such a successful son and so natural to want everyone to like him. Although the engagement had been a surprise, Emma was pleased for her son and eager to meet his fiancée.

Fay had not met Anthony, they had spoken often on the phone and in a small way she felt she already knew him. She frowned, 'I hope Emma approves of Leona,' she thought. Though fond of her employer she also knew how difficult she could be if someone was not to her liking or things didn't go her way.

Glancing at the clock, she grimaced. Unless she hurried, there would be no time to get herself ready. Turning to her computer Fay started typing the last chapter of the new book. Soon she was engrossed and wondering where her employer got the material for her crime thrillers. There was always so much detail in them which made them plausible and good to read. There it was, finished, time to go.

Chapter 2

Checking her image in the mirror, Fay frowned and tugged at her unruly hair. The mirrored image was of an attractive young girl, fair hair tinged with auburn and cut in a style to frame her slim heart-shaped face. She had not long been back from a weekend break in Spain where she had relaxed, topping up her tan. Most people would not call her stunning, but with her classic features, slim figure and pleasant personality she attracted her fair share of attention from the young men on the island.

The green dress she had chosen to wear showed off her tanned skin and the colour seemed to reflect the green of her eyes. It was made of a light material that appeared to shimmer as Fay moved. The cleverly cut design made the dress cling to her body showing her figure to perfection. High-heeled silver sandals added a look of elegance to her dress.

She was never happy with her appearance, and tonight wasn't any different. Fay looked at her reflection and shook her head. 'Well, it's the best I can do'.

Picking up her bag and a light lacy shawl she walked out to her car, totally unaware just how attractive she actually looked.

It was November. In England it would be quite cold now, but in Gibraltar the evenings were still warm. It always gave Fay a thrill to recall winters in England. The crisp frost and virgin snow making strange patterns on fences and ponds, long icicles hanging from gutters forming strange spikes which took so long to melt and made strange forms as they dripped away and changed shape. Sometimes she missed the crisp snowy winter walks she used to take, and the sight of her breath freezing as she breathed out.

Fay, along with most of the residents of Gibraltar, accepted the awful storms that pounded the island on occasions, and revelled in the balmy evenings and sunny days that sometimes seemed as if they would go on forever. Recent storms had caused a lot of damage especially to the water catchments. Water was a valuable commodity here so any damage to the catchments was serious and a worry for the island's residents.

'Good, there are still plenty of spaces', she thought as she pulled into the parking lot. Thank goodness the dinner was here tonight; parking in Gibraltar was always a problem. There was an aviary in the garden linking the casino, hotel and the car park, which she always liked walking through. Sometimes the birds would wake and bring song to the evening. Fay would stop and listen, then on taking her leave, she mouth a word of apology to the birds for disturbing their sleep.

The garden had a vaguely Victorian feel just like the hotel next to the casino. She had often sat sipping cocktails, imagining men in evening suits and ladies in beautiful Victorian ball gowns enjoying polite conversation in the garden. Sometimes she would imagine she could hear an orchestra playing a Viennese waltz and would close her eyes trying to visualize the ladies in those wonderful gowns and the men looking so handsome in their resplendent regalia, dancing around the ballroom.

The hotel was large, from the windows you could see the boats moored in the harbour and in the distance the Spanish coastline. It had a subtle air of grandeur whilst still retaining a welcoming atmosphere. Its reputation as the best hotel in Gibraltar was, in her opinion, justified. The restaurant and service were excellent but it was the spectacular views that always impressed her the most.

Spotting her as she crossed the hotel foyer, Emma smiled and beckoned Fay to hurry and join her. 'Looking perfect as usual,' Emma thought. 'I would like to know why she has never been in a serious relationship since coming to here; it wasn't due to lack of opportunity.'

It was obvious from the relaxed atmosphere and the smile on Emma's face that Leona had already made a good impression, Fay smiled and let out a silent sigh.

"You look lovely. Come and meet my son and his fiancé." Emma said, taking Fay's arm.

"Anthony, Leona, this is Fay my friend and invaluable assistant."

As the couple turned to greet her, Fay smiled. Anthony reached out and took her hand.

"I am delighted to meet you at last. It is nice to have a face to fit the voice and one that is just as lovely as it sounded."

Fay smiled and thought how like his mother Anthony was. Obviously he had inherited her ability to charm when he wished. Hmm, he's not exactly handsome she thought, but there was an openness about him which made her like him instantly.

"Thank you. I did have the advantage as I had seen photos of you, although they did not do you justice."

Holding her hand out she greeted Leona. "So pleased to meet you. How was your journey?"

"Nice to meet you too, Fay. The journey was very good, though the landing was a little daunting, I had no idea how short the runway is," Leona smiled. "Anthony has spoken of you Fay, I feel as if I already know you."

A man was standing slightly behind Leona. Fay hadn't noticed him until he stepped forward so that he could be introduced. Leona turned, linking her arm though his as she spoke, "Let me introduce you to Nathan Mackenzie, a good friend of ours."

"Pleased to meet you, Mr Mackenzie." Fay shook the proffered hand.

"Please call me Nathan, and the pleasure is mine. Anthony has spoken of you, it is nice to put a face to your name." he replied smiling as he shook her hand.

It was the smile that did it. She felt certain that everyone would have noticed. Trying to hide her inner turmoil Fay glanced around. Thank goodness no one seemed to have noticed her blush or the fact that her legs had turned to jelly when Nathan shook her hand.

For a second she was totally wrong footed. It had been a long time since a man had affected her this way; in fact not since Thomas, and he was the first. It was a feeling she was not sure she wanted reminding of and one she had sworn not to fall foul of again.

Attempting to recover her composure, Fay turned to Leona. "Anthony should have warned you about the landing strip, some people find it quite scary."

Leona laughed. "Actually I am not the greatest traveller but on this occasion I was so looking forward to meeting Emma that I would not have taken any notice if he had."

Emma smiled, "And I, my dear, was more than eager to see my son's fiancé. Now how long do I have to wait to see your dress; till the day or can I have a peek earlier?"

Leona's face lit up. "Well it seems to have travelled quite well. I unpacked it as soon as we arrived and hung it in the bathroom to allow any creases to drop out." She paused and nibbled her lip, "I would like you to see it at its best. Oh, I don't see any reason you can't see it, perhaps later in the week."

"I can't wait and I am sure it will be perfect, Leona." Emma smiled and turned her attention to Nathan.

Leona looked across at Fay. "Actually I was wondering if you could spare some time to take me shopping? There are still one or two things I need and Anthony assured me I could get them here. He thought you might be the person to help me."

"Of course I can, I would really enjoy that provided my employer can do without me for a couple of hours." She smiled in Emma's direction knowing full well that there would be no problem.

The waiter arrived with their champagne cocktails. Fay picked up her glass and joined in the toast to the happy couple. The conversation turned into a discussion on wedding arrangements. Whilst everyone was busy talking Fay turned to look out over the bay.

The view from the hotel was superb, she never tired of it. Normally it had a calming restful effect on her but tonight she was feeling on edge. Nathan was filling her thoughts. 'Stop behaving like a school girl,' she chided herself. Then she caught Nathan's reflection in the window as he chatted with the others. It was difficult to read. His face in repose was serious, even closed and solitary. Perhaps to stop people getting too close, a feeling she knew only too well. Damn! She couldn't help recalling his devastating smile and the feel of his hand holding hers.

Just then Nathan turned to look over the bay. Lost in his own thoughts he didn't notice Fay's reflection as she watched him.

Six foot tall with black hair and hazel eyes, he made a striking figure. Add to that his tan and the dinner jacket, he reminded her of a fictional character in one of Emma's detective novels.

I wonder what his story is? He is certainly very handsome. She halted her train of thought before it went too far, and taking one more quick glance at Nathan's reflection, she turned and rejoined the group.

Chapter 3

Had anyone been looking at the window they would have seen, just for a moment, the reflections of Nathan and Fay mirrored in the glass, both sharing the same wary, 'don't get too close' expression.

Her feelings about Nathan being solitary and distant were nearer the truth than Fay knew. He had experienced personal tragedy and in an effort to avoid being hurt again he held most people at a distance. His friends were few, all people who liked him and respected his feelings, although not all knew the reasons for them.

Nathan had been married for just over eight months when his wife told him she was pregnant. They were both overjoyed and started making all the usual plans for their new arrival. He couldn't wait to meet his child who would make his life complete. Lou seemed to blossom and their relationship had never been so good. They made plans and spent endless hours discussing what the future held for them as a family. Everything seemed perfect. Then as the time went on and the birth got nearer, Lou began to feel unwell. Somehow she knew things weren't right. They spoke to the doctor who was looking after her. He suggested they see another consultant and arranged an urgent appointment. It was only matter of days before their bubble of happiness was burst.

Lou had developed cancer and ran the risk of losing her life if she continued with the pregnancy. She refused to terminate the pregnancy and kill their child. 'How could our happiness be complete without our child?' she had asked Nathan. Despite his constantly telling her she was his world, he couldn't envisage life without her. There was no reason why they couldn't try for another child when she was well, but Lou had refused all treatment. She wanted to have her baby first then she would begin treatment.

Both Lou and the baby died soon after the birth. There had been only a couple of hours for him to name his son and then say goodbye to Lou and Duncan within minutes of each other. Nathan had never felt so desolate, he retreated into himself allowing no one to help him accept his loss, isolating himself completely.

That was only 18 months ago, and Nathan was still coming to terms with losing his family. He blamed himself, mostly for going along with Lou's wishes; he should have tried harder to persuade her to start the treatment immediately. Deep down he knew Lou would have fought him all the way, making their last few weeks together even harder and more miserable.

Nathan's despair nearly drove him crazy, he had never felt so lost and empty. His devastation was completely overwhelming. After the funeral he returned to work, volunteering for more and more assignments, regardless of where they were or how dangerous they might be. It was meeting Anthony at a gym that had started the healing process. They had started chatting one day when the gym was quiet, and gradually over a few weeks they became friends. Their friendship was now one of the stable elements in Nathan's life.

As he looked out over the bay his mind was on his work and the reason he was here. Drugs were being smuggled into England and the trail led to Gibraltar. He'd been asked if he would lead the undercover investigation for his department. He knew it was a difficult and potentially dangerous assignment because of the people believed to be involved. He accepted the assignment feeling he had nothing to risk, unlike his married colleagues.

Shortly afterwards, Anthony told him he was getting married and wanted Nathan to be his best man. The ceremony would be in Gibraltar. So Nathan found himself on the island for work at the same time as being best man for Anthony and

Leona. Not ideal, but for some reason, when he told his boss that he could be compromising his cover and the job by being seen with his personal friends, he had made light of it.

"Just make sure they don't get involved, after all we are not sure this information is solid. It could be a wild goose chase, in which case you can stay over, have a break."

Nathan was surprised as it was a strict rule not to involve civilians especially if things looked like they could get nasty. This assignment was more than a little tricky; still, if his Chief was happy, who was he to argue? Even so he was not comfortable with the knowledge that his friends were going to be there whilst he was working on the island.

Nathan knew this job was not going to be an easy one. People imported drugs from anywhere these days, having moved them through an assortment of countries. The group allegedly moving them through Gibraltar were thought to play in the major league. They were people who undoubtedly knew all the wrinkles and anyone informing or interfering in their plans would be in great danger.

A sudden movement in the window caught his eye and his gaze shifted slightly. He saw the back of Fay's reflection in the window which brought his mind back to the celebrations. Fay was quite a surprise; Emma's assistant. Well, that made her sound like a 50-something P.A. with glasses and grey hair, certainly not like the young lively girl he had been introduced to. She was very attractive, young, fair haired and he hadn't noticed her wearing glasses. She was obviously English and he'd noticed she didn't wear a ring on her left hand, so presumably she was single. She seemed young to be unattached and so far from her homeland.

Looking out to the bay, his mind went back to the investigation. He hated this situation; friendships should be kept separate from work, but he couldn't see how it was to be avoided on this occasion. His only concern was that things didn't get messy, he didn't want Anthony and Leona involved.

Anthony was his closest friend and had helped him more than he knew during the past months. When Anthony introduced him to Leona at the gym, he felt a little uncertain how their friendship would be affected but Leona had very quickly become a friend to him as well. He had not expected things to move so quickly and was surprised when they told him they were getting married, although he thought she was a perfect partner for Anthony. He hoped they would be as happy as he and Lou had been. Nathan sighed, suddenly he felt very alone.

He couldn't help but think that his reason for being here could impact on the wedding. Enough, he told himself, all this can wait till tomorrow when I hear from my contact. Tonight is Anthony and Leona's evening. Until he had more information he could not be sure of anything anyway. He turned and rejoined the group.

Chapter 4

They finished their cocktails and left the hotel to walk the short distance to the casino. "I feel lucky tonight," said Emma. "Hopefully you youngsters will bring me good fortune," she smiled vaguely in the direction of Anthony and Leona.

What a relief. It looked as if Emma liked Leona, so the only fireworks to be lit would be on the wedding day. Fay stopped to look at the birds, who raised their heads as if telling her off for waking them again. She smiled to herself and felt sorry for them always being caged. In the half-light she was startled by the unexpected voice close behind and jumped in surprise. There was no need to look to see who it was, her pulses were already racing.

"It's a shame to wake them. Do you wonder what they dream about in their gilded cages?" Nathan smiled as Fay turned to face him.

My goodness he is tall, and too close. Come on, get a grip, she told herself. "Gilded cage it may be, but they are well cared for. Maybe they think we are the ones in the cages."

Nathan looked into her upturned face and thought how lovely she was. Really quite enchanting he thought, not at all what he had expected when he was told Emma's assistant would be at the welcome dinner. Then his mind took over, shutting out any further thoughts that could lead him in that direction.

"I don't like to see anything wild, caged. They were born to fly free and that's how I like to see them." He stepped back a little, her closeness was disturbing. "Having said that, I would agree there are certain occasions when cages are appropriate."

"Shall we join the others? They'll think we are lost." He turned and stepped back waiting for her to step in front of him and walk on towards the casino.

For a brief moment as she had looked up into his face, he had felt the urge to take her hand. He felt somehow that she was lost, uncertain and in need of reassurance.

Maybe they both had experienced things which had caused chaos in their lives. He felt a sudden closeness of a kindred spirit, something he had not felt for a long, long time. Then he felt annoyed that this girl who he'd only just met, should be the cause of these feelings that had unexpectedly surfaced.

Fay had seen the sudden change in his expression, she wondered what had caused it. Something seemed to annoy him yet she couldn't think what it could be. Was it something I said? But going over her words, she could not find anything that would cause offence.

As they continued the walk to the casino, both were lost in their thoughts. Nathan trying to put the memories that his encounter with Fay had caused to resurface, back in their box. He had not felt the slightest interest in any female since Lou's death and yet somewhere deep inside he knew he was drawn to this girl.

He sensed that despite her friendly, open personality she too held people at arm's length. There was an invisible protective shell around her just like the one he had built round himself.

'I'll have to be a bit more guarded with her', he thought. He had no desire to get involved with anyone, especially as his work could place them in danger if he was not careful. Hopefully once the wedding was over they would have no need to come into contact again. His mind took a sharp turn reminding him of the reason for him building his own barrier.

He mentally shook himself, not wanting to analyse the thoughts that would bring the hurt he had buried so deep inside himself to the surface.

Glancing at Fay as she walked ahead, he noticed how the moon played on her hair, making it shine as if it was threaded with silvery strands, and how it emphasised her slim figure. No, not at all the image he had of an author's personal assistant, he thought.

They stepped into the lift but neither spoke as it took them up to the casino. As they emerged from the lift into the outer gaming area, he watched as she walked ahead. Well, her protective shell is not my problem, attractive as she was, he was not about to get interested.

The dinner party was going well. It was so large it was difficult to speak to everyone. In fact it appeared to Fay that half the island had been invited. Emma was well known and liked, so her son's forthcoming wedding was greeted with pleasure by her friends. Leona and Anthony were sociable people and seemed to be making a favourable impression, whilst Emma had a broad smile on her face almost permanently.

Nathan, it seemed, was also making an impression, mainly on the single women in the party. Gossip had already got back to her that he was thought to be very good looking, slightly dangerous but worth the challenge. It was a good job he was not planning to stay, she thought. He was causing a stir amongst her friends as well as unsettling her.

She was absorbed in watching her friend's reactions, when Nathan asked her to dance. Fay was surprised by Nathan's invitation as he had said little to her since they arrived at the casino. As they stepped onto the floor she could feel several pairs of envious eyes watching them. If only they knew how fast my heart is beating, she thought, they might be more than envious.

He was a good dancer which for some reason surprised her. It was a while before they returned to the table, laughing and in need of refreshment. Almost as soon as they sat down, Anthony asked her to dance, and with so many of her own friends at the dinner, from then on she was hardly off the floor.

Fay felt flushed and went out onto the balcony for some air, although it wasn't the heat that was making her hot, or the dancing. She had felt so safe in Nathan's arms and instinctively she knew this was a man whose friendship she could value, someone she could trust.

'Remember Thomas? You thought the same about him and look what happened.' This subconscious thought brought her down with a jolt. The last person she wished to remember was Thomas. I think I will forget dancing and try my luck on the tables, she decided. Perhaps my reaction to Nathan was due to the occasion. After all, romance was in the air tonight. She turned and walked back to join Emma, who was already playing roulette. Taking a seat, she looked around, watching other players before decided to play. She'd noticed that Nathan, Anthony and Leona seemed deep in discussion, seemingly not interested in the gambling. Discussing the wedding, no doubt, although by now it was pretty much organised.

At first both Emma and Fay were winning, then after a while her pile of chips began to shrink. Fay decided that she would quit while she was ahead, and that her next bet would be the last of the evening. Reaching forward to place some chips, she felt a hand rest lightly on her shoulder. Looking up she found herself gazing into hazel eyes.

"I feel lucky tonight, try my favourite numbers and see if they work for you," Nathan said, smiling in a most unnerving way.

She felt herself flush "OK, what the heck! You might just bring me some luck." Placing her bet she smiled at him, "This is my last one anyway, then I'm off home."

The croupier was a friend of Fay's. She had been out with him a couple of times. He'd wanted to be more than a friend but she had made it clear that wasn't going to happen. He had accepted this and was fine with keeping their relationship on an informal basis. He was, however, one of her closer friends and had been pleased to see her winning. She placed her chips watching the wheel spin and as the clipping of the ball stopped, she was pleased to see she'd won.

Smiling, the croupier pushed the chips towards her. "Your luck was in tonight madam."

Fay felt that although he was addressing her he was looking at Nathan. She leant forward to pick up her chips. "Thanks Jerry, I think I will quit while I am ahead."

"You brought me luck, Nathan. Can I buy you a drink from my ill-gotten gains?"

"Thanks, but it has been a long day. I'm beginning to feel tired. I think I will be heading for my bed soon. However, I will come and cash your chips in with you."

I wish he didn't have such a killer smile, Fay thought as she turned to Emma.

"What about you Emma?"

"I might stay a little longer. Honestly, you youngsters have no stamina." She laughed as she turned back to the table hoping her luck would hold out a little bit longer.

"OK then, I'll be off, thank you for a lovely evening.!

"I'll pick Leona up about nine in the morning for our shopping trip." Fay smiled, "Don't lose too much."

Only someone very observant would have noticed that the croupier was watching Fay and Nathan closely as they left the room.

Emma was observant and noticed his interest. She didn't know too much about Jerry. He had never really caught her attention until he made friends with Fay. He'd always been polite and seemed a decent sort. Maybe he is jealous, he's taken Fay out a fair bit, she thought, but somehow she didn't think it was Fay he was watching. Then again, who else could it have been. There was something a bit odd about him tonight but she couldn't put her finger on what it was. Just then the croupier asked her if she was placing a bet. Smiling, she put chips down and turned her mind back to the game.

After cashing her chips in, Fay thanked Nathan again for bringing her luck.

"Will you be at the house tomorrow?" she asked as they headed towards the lift.

He shook his head. "I have some business to attend to. Would you like me to escort you and your winnings to the car?"

"No, that's fine. Goodnight, I hope you sleep well."

Fay stepped into the lift and as the doors closed she felt a feeling of relief sweep over her. She could relax and stop trying to control her feelings now. She had felt like a silly schoolgirl ever since Nathan had joined her at the tables.

As she walked to the car her mind was buzzing, going over the evening's events. The cool night air was comforting after the heat of the casino and she walked slowly enjoying the change of temperature. Suddenly she felt uneasy, stopping she stood still looking back over her shoulder to the entrance and then looking around the rest of the car park. No one in sight, nothing there to worry about. It must be my imagination, she told herself, trying to ignore the apprehension which had begun to disturb her. I'm just tired.

Reaching her car she got the car key from her bag, half looking back as she turned the key in the lock. It was then she heard a movement behind her, turning quickly she looked into the shadows. A figure emerged from the darkness, making her heart race in fright. She tugged at the car door to get inside to safety.

The door was only half open when she heard hurried steps as someone walked across the gravelled ground. She began to feel vulnerable and wished now she had let Nathan walk her to the car. Suddenly a man stepped forward from the shadows into the dim light of the car park. As he came in to full view Fay almost cried out in shock.

It can't be, she thought, then recognition hit her. She backed away from the man, colliding with the half-open car door, shaking her head in disbelief.

He walked towards her, holding out a hand as if reaching for her. Even in the dim light he could see she was shocked and frightened by his sudden appearance.

"Fay, I'm sorry. I saw you in the casino and wanted to speak to you alone. Please, I didn't mean to frighten you." He moved towards her still holding out his hand. "It's me, Thomas. Don't you recognize me?"

Oh, she had recognized him all right, but the shock of seeing him seemed to render her speechless.

The sound of his voice mobilised her. Questions were rushing through her head, courses of action she could take to escape from him. One thought was uppermost, the need to get away from him.

"Stay away from me!" she shouted as he moved closer, his hands still outstretched. She was sure he was going to grab her and moved quickly to get to hold of the car door handle. "What are you doing here? Have you been watching me?" As she spoke, Fay pulled the handle and slid into the opening, putting the car door between, them fearing he might try to prevent her getting away.

As Thomas got closer, Fay felt a tremor of fear run through her, and still shaking and confused, she kept a tight hold of the car door. He was moving closer to the car and reached out to her. She pushed his arms away before he could get hold of her, angrily shouting out as he resisted her attempts to stop him touching her.

"Go away, whatever your reasons for being here I don't want to know. When I told you I never wanted to see or hear from you again I meant it, nothing has changed. Stay away and never bother me again." With a shrug of despair she slid into the car seat and reached for the ignition.

"I mean it Thomas, stay away from me."

Thomas reached for the door handle but she managed to lock the door before he could pull it open. Panicking she turned the key hoping the engine wouldn't stall.

Slamming the car into gear she reversed. Thomas was still holding the door handle but Fay did not care if he was dragged along by the car.

The sound of the racing engine didn't drown out the sound of Thomas shouting as he lost his grip and fell. The car screeched as she raced out of the car park, skidding on the loose gravel. Looking back in her mirror she saw him get up and run after the car, then he stopped and stood, looking into the darkness as she drove off as fast as she could.

Fay knew she was driving too fast, taking the corners too quickly as she drove up the hill, desperate to get away from him. It was only when she reached her house the shock took over. As she pulled up outside, Fay felt hot tears running over her cheeks, shaking with fear and relief. She had managed to avoid Thomas.

Angrily brushing the tears away, she tried to gather her thoughts. Unable to let go of the steering wheel, she sat in the car; somehow it seemed her only protection. I must get inside, she thought. He might have followed me. She glanced in her mirror just in case he was there.

Then the memories started to flood her mind. Memories she had worked hard to bury so long ago. Fay wasn't sure if they could still hurt her, but tonight she had been frightened by Thomas suddenly appearing and she knew they could. How could he be here, why was he here and what did he want? The questions just kept coming and with no answers she was getting more and more confused and upset.

Well, whatever he wants I want nothing to do with him. He was and always will be a lying, cheating creep, and he would not have changed, of that she was certain. A nightmare from the past, that's all Thomas was, a nightmare she had conquered years ago; at least she thought she had.

The flow of tears had stopped and left her eyes smarting. Seeing him tonight had given her a big jolt. Feeling a little calmer, Fay got out of the car and let herself into her house, checking again that no one was in sight.

Old memories and emotions were now surfacing quickly. Images from the past springing to the surface unbidden and unwanted. Emotions she had thought dead, forgotten, now filled her mind forcing her to face feelings she had never wanted to deal with all those years ago. Memories which she had kept buried for so long now surfaced.

Suddenly the question she most dreaded sprang clearly into her head. Surely I can't still love him? No, she shook her head in denial, no, never, not after what he did.

Chapter 5

Suddenly Fay was back in England reliving events that had happened three years ago. Then she had been blissfully happy, unaware of what was to come. She felt a cold shiver of shock and apprehension run through her. Stop it, stop trying to analyse your feelings. Once again she tried to halt her thoughts but her mind refused to let go and pushed her back to the night their relationship had come to an end.

It was a lovely summers evening and Fay had prepared a celebration dinner for them, making all Thomas's favourite dishes. He had proposed the previous night and loving him as she did, she had no hesitation in accepting. Thomas had said he would like her to have his mother's ring and would bring it over tonight. Everything had to be perfect, the weather was good, the meal was cooking, the table looked splendid. Yes, she had thought, tonight was going to be perfect. Tonight, Thomas was going to stay, they would be creating a memory which would be special and remembered into their old age.

Thomas arrived punctually as usual with flowers and champagne. He had been there about 15 minutes when, as she was about to suggest they start their meal, the doorbell rang.

He told her to see to the meal as he went to answer the door. She put several dishes on the table then went to see what was keeping him. As she walked into the hall she heard raised voices and was just in time to see Thomas in a scuffle with a woman. It looked as if he was trying to push her out of the door.

The woman saw Fay and smiled. Pushing harder against the door she shouted, "So this is your love interest, is it darling?" Her smile was hard and insincere. "What has happened to your manners? Introduce me to your mistress, Thomas."

As he turned to look at Fay, the women took her opportunity and pushed the door open, catching Thomas off balance as she pushed past him and walked towards Fay.

She looked so elegant but her voice was angry, icy. As Fay looked at her she felt sent a shiver of apprehension. The woman directed her cold angry gaze towards her, looking directly at Fay as she spoke.

Her face was full of malice, her eyes cold and hard, Fay could remember even now how threatened she had felt by this stranger.

Looking at Thomas for some sort of explanation, Fay was shocked by the expression on his face. He never moved, never spoke, just stood in the open doorway. He looked defeated and was shaking, seemingly unable to do or say anything.

The woman smiled. "Lost your tongue darling? Well let me speak for you." Thomas's face turned white, his expression to one of anger but still he said nothing.

"Allow me to introduce myself." she said, walking closer to Fay and staring her in the face.

"Forgive me for barging in my dear, but I'm sure my name is not on your invitation list. My name is Debra and I am his wife." She nodded her head in Thomas's direction.

"Oh, you look shocked. Well that won't wash with me. You must have known he was married; your sort always does. If you play with fire you should expect to get burnt." Debra pointed her finger at Fay, so close she almost prodded her. "Believe me, he is definitely fire."

Fay stepped back in an effort to get away from this angry woman but found she was trapped by the dining room door.

"Don't think you're special. You are not the first, I assure you." The woman laughed and then continued with a look of pure malice. "I've wanted a divorce for ages but he always managed to talk his way out of it, but not this time; this time I will be rid of him for good."

Debra turned slightly, looking over her shoulder at Thomas who had not moved from the door. He appeared to be dumb struck.

"I'm citing her as the other woman," she pointed at Fay, "I will get you out of my life at last. Don't expect to see either of us again, I will be asking for sole custody. Not that you ever were much of a father."

Turning back to Fay she sneered. "Thank you my dear. You have done me a big favour, I hope you will be happy. Personally I am glad to see the back of him. I expect in time you will too."

Debra turned and stepped out of the door.

"I'd love to stay for a long chat but as I said, I didn't receive an invitation. You'll both be sure to accept mine for the court hearing won't you." She laughed hysterically as she walked down the path after slamming the door behind her.

There was a moment's silence then Thomas kicked the door viscously as if he was kicking the women who had just left. He stood with his back to Fay for a few seconds, then turned and walked towards her.

"I can explain Fay, let me explain," he held out his hand as if to pull her to him. "Please Fay, don't look at me like that. She hasn't got grounds for citing you, she's just bluffing."

"Don't, Thomas," she said evading his hands. "Please just tell me it isn't true; that woman is not your wife." Fay pleaded with him, still unable to understand what was happening, yet somewhere deep in her mind she knew every word the women had spoken was true.

The sound of Debra's cruel laughter was still ringing in her ears. Her sneering smile stuck in Fay's mind and her obvious delight that at last she had caught Thomas out confirmed her story.

He shook his head and began to blurt out words which were meant to convince her that Debra was lying. All he achieved was a lot of blustering sentences which did not make sense and sounded absurd. His voice was pleading but insincere, his face wore an expression of anger mixed with fear. He was only reinforcing what had been said with every word he spoke.

She cut him short, there was no way he could deny the facts, she realised that now. Debra, that dreadful, angry, bitter, triumphant women was indeed his wife. Her whole future had been built on shifting sand, their relationship had been a complete sham of lies and deceit.

Thomas stopped talking and was looking at her, waiting for her to react. She felt sick and used. All the evenings he had wanted to stay overnight; thank goodness she had insisted he leave. He would have been her first lover and she had wanted things to be special.

The irony was that she had decided that tonight would be that special occasion; well, it was special all right, they were through.

'No Grounds', his words came back to her; more by luck than judgement! She felt ashamed as she started to take in the enormity of his actions and realised how foolish she had been.

Fay had leant on the hall table for support during Debra's tirade, now as she moved she felt the ring box, brushing against her hand. Picking up the box she looked at Thomas and shouted,

"Get out, just get out and take this with you."

He flinched as the box hit his face.

The despair in her voice seemed to shock him into action and he moved towards her again.

"Fay please, please listen............." he said.

Finally it was sinking in, at last Fay lost her hold over her emotions, tears were threatening to fall. Evading his embrace she calmly told him to go. "Get out now or I will call the police. Go and don't ever come back. I never want to see or hear from you again."

His hand went to his face where the ring box had left a red mark. He bent down to pick it up. He looked at her for a moment then turned to the door.

"OK, I'll go but we will talk in the morning." As he reached the bottom step he turned and looked back at her. "We can sort this out, really we can. I will call you tomorrow."

Fay had slammed the door in his face. Then as her tears started to fall she turned and saw the phone. Bending down she pulled the lead from the wall. She had no intention of sorting anything out with him tonight, tomorrow or next year! That was that, until tonight.

Chapter 6

Thomas had tried all ways to contact her. When he realised she had disconnected her phone, he called in person but she ignored the doorbell and kept her curtains drawn.

His letters were thrown away unopened. If she saw him in the street she would walk in the opposite direction as quickly as possible and if he followed her, she would hide in the nearest shop until he had gone.

Her decision had been made on that dreadful night. There was no one now to keep her here; her friends were few and more acquaintances than friends, they would not miss her. She made all the arrangements as quickly as she could. Getting as far away as possible from Thomas was the only way she could move on. She started by looking for a job abroad.

Emma's advert was perfectly timed and once the job had been confirmed she moved, leaving estate agents to deal with the sale of her house.

The move to Gibraltar was meant to be a new start. Thomas was out of her life, just a painful but distant fading memory. A lesson learned and she had learnt it well – but now he was back.

The tears started to fall again, and angrily she wiped them away. Why had he come back into her life? She was over him, he would complicate things, once again painful memories were filling her head.

The house felt cold and she began to feel the tension in her body. She was emotionally wrung out but her tears were abating. I need a drink, she thought, and stepping over her bag which had dropped to the floor, she walked into the lounge.

Pouring a brandy, she sat down, feeling a heavy cloud was descending on her and overshadowing her life.

Surely he would not bother her again; he must have been in no doubt she did not want to see him again. Eventually her eyes, swollen from her tears began to droop and she fell into an uneasy sleep in the chair.

Waking with a start, Fay couldn't make out what the noise in her head was. She wished it would stop, it sounded so far away but was very insistent. Eventually the ringing phone penetrated her brain. What on earth? In an instant she recalled the events of the previous evening and realised why she was asleep in a chair and fully dressed. The insistent ringing dragged her back to reality.

'Oh no! I should be taking Leona shopping. She glanced at the clock. It was 9.30 am. Damn! She jumped up and answered the phone.

"Hello?" She tried to sound normal and not as if she had just woken up.

Emma was worried. She had tried Fay's number twice and got no reply. It's not like her to be late. I hope she is OK. She frowned and was just about to replace the receiver on the third attempt when Fay answered.

"Fay, it's Emma, are you all right? I've been ringing for ages."

"I'm sorry Emma, I was in the shower, didn't hear the phone." Fay lied. "I've overslept... be there as soon as possible." She replaced the receiver before any further questions could be asked.

That's the first time I have lied to Emma, she thought. Thomas's charm was poisonous as she well knew and now it was infecting her new life.

As she turned to go upstairs to get ready, Fay caught sight of herself in the mirror. Her face was pale and she looked exhausted. With a sigh she realised it was going to be difficult to convince Emma that nothing was wrong.

'Pull yourself together,' she murmured. Thomas has probably gone. After all, he had not received much of a welcome. As she thought over their meeting she did feel he was genuinely surprised to see her last night, so her fear that he had come to find her could be unfounded.

He has probably completed his business and would be leaving the island today, in which case she would not see him again. Fay kept thinking positively, attempting to convince herself that Thomas was again in her past.

Sitting looking around her home it was as if the familiar surroundings could offer comfort. Then catching sight of the clock, she realised how late she was and rushed up the stairs to step into the shower.

Emma was no one's fool. Fay knew that she must hide her anxiety, or explanations would be needed. Emma was protective of her friends and would be angry and concerned if anyone hurt her, but most of all she did not want to explain to her about last night or why it had upset her so much. She was still trying to understand it herself.

At times it seemed that Emma had accepted her as the daughter she had lost before Anthony was born. There was a photograph on Emma's desk of Angel. Fay commented on how pretty the child was and Emma had told her that it was her daughter who had died in tragic circumstances but said no more. Sensing that this was a taboo subject, Fay never mentioned it again. She knew only too well there were things in everyone's life they did not want to relive.

Dressing quickly, she looked round for her keys, finding them eventually on the floor in the hall, then recalled how upset she had been the previous evening. Shaking her head as if to clear it, she went out to her car. Driving to pick up Leona, Fay thought that maybe it would be something of a distraction for her today. Maybe a few hours with Leona shopping would help her forget last night's events, or at least put them in perspective.

Leona was waiting for Fay, eager to get on with her shopping.

"Hi, are you OK?" she asked. "Emma was worried. It's not like you to sleep in."

"I'm fine, just overslept and then couldn't get myself going; not used to these late nights. Sorry to keep you waiting. Let's go, I'm in the mood for some retail therapy."

They waved to Anthony and Emma who had appeared at the study window. Fay did not want to stop and speak to them; she needed to escape Emma's sharp eyes.

As she watched them drive away, Emma frowned. Something is wrong. I know that girl like my own and she is not herself. It had taken some time for Emma to think of Fay as more than an employee. She sensed there was something in her past which she was keeping to herself, but then as they got to know each other it didn't matter. Emma was a good judge of character and Fay would never be questioned by her. Emma also realised that she had let her fill a little of the void that losing Angel had left.

Still, something did not add up. Emma knew how much importance Fay put on being reliable and her timekeeping was usually excellent. She had sounded tired and out of sorts on the phone. Ah well, no good me worrying, most things become clear, given time.

Chapter 7

Emma was going over last evening in detail, something she did since starting to write and now it was just routine. Fortunate really, it was how she worked, checking every detail, trying to ensure there were no mistakes when a case reached the court.

It had been a nice evening, everyone seemed to enjoy themselves and Leona was an instant hit. She had liked her within a few minutes of meeting her, and was so pleased for her son that he had found a beautiful girl, both in looks and nature.

She did feel that they were rushing things a bit, but then youngsters always seemed in a hurry these days. It was nice to win on the tables too, rounding the evening off perfectly.

She frowned, 'I wonder what connection there is between Nathan and the croupier?' Nathan had not seemed to know him but somehow she felt the croupier was watching Nathan closely. Her mind did a flip and she found herself thinking about her current investigation.

Inspector Luchiano was an old friend, had been since Frank had been killed. Soon after the death of her family she joined the police force, believing she would find their killers. Now she worked directly for Luchiano and Emma knew he had grown to respect her instincts and judgement.

Currently the police and customs were working together on a possible case of smuggling that could involve drugs and arms passing through the island.

Why must it always be those two things? Serious crimes, and yet the criminals seemed to elude everyone so easily. Luchiano had told her that she would be informed when to meet her contact from the mainland, but so far nothing had happened.

Her mind began to run free and eventually returned her to that awful day when her husband Frank had taken their daughter off for a walk, which neither of them had survived.

They had moved to Gibraltar soon after their marriage. Frank worked for the police but would never discuss his work with her. "It's too sordid Em, you really are better not knowing", he would say when she questioned him. Had she known how dangerous his role in the force was she may not have let him take their daughter anywhere, let alone without her by their side.

Then again what life would they have had? At least Anthony grew up in comparative safety. She sighed and let her thoughts run on.

Frank had been working on a case which was nearing its conclusion. One night when he got home, Angel was being fractious and Emma was beginning to lose patience with her. After the day he'd just had, he needed to clear his head so suggested he took Angel for a walk. She remembered agreeing with a sense of relief that she could get a moment's peace. Calling over her shoulder, "Love you both lot's", she heard the door click as it shut behind them.

It was about an hour later when the doorbell rang, and as she went to answer it she suddenly felt a deep sense of apprehension. The caller was Frank's Chief with one of his female colleagues.

"May we come in Emma?" he asked. She stood back and let them pass, shutting the door and walking after them into the lounge. One of them asked her to sit down. She had remained standing.

"Emma, I am afraid there has been an incident in which Frank and Angel were involved. They are both in hospital; I am sorry to tell you that their injuries are serious," the Chief looked pale and worried. "We would like you to come immediately. There is a car waiting outside."

She had just stared at him, thinking this can't be right, they've just gone for a walk, they will be back anytime.

Nodding, she picked up her house keys then walked out to the car, still not having spoken a word. When they got into the car she asked what had happened and was told they would discuss this with her later, but right now she was needed at the hospital.

Angel died in her arms and Frank only lived long enough to tell her how much he loved her and he was so sorry. Sorry for what, she had asked but he had gone. Never knowing he was to be a father again, never to meet his son.

Eventually Emma found out that Frank had been working on a drugs case and from the information the police had, he got too close and someone arranged an 'accident'. Angel was caught up in the incident. The culprits had never been found.

That's when she understood why Frank had said he was sorry. He knew she would not have been happy for him to be involved in such dangerous work and would have been more protective of him and Angel.

So there she was, 24 years old with a child on the way and emotionally wrecked by her double loss. Being pregnant helped her find something to live for. Thank goodness there were also many good friends to support her. Luchiano and his family were among those who helped her rebuild her life.

Soon Emma began writing, usually crime stories that nearly always involved drugs. It helped her financially and filled her time so that she did not slip into a depressed state of mind.

Her books had to be right, so she spent a lot of time checking details and spoke to as many experts on drug crime as she could. She had become somewhat of an expert on local crime and then found herself joining the police, eventually working as an undercover operative. Her knowledge of the island and the people was invaluable and her popularity amongst the locals meant she could get information the police couldn't, albeit done in the name of research for her next book.

It was exciting to be working undercover. Anthony was grown up and although there was the occasional risk, she really enjoyed this hidden side of her life. Somehow her work filled the enormous gap left by losing two of the people she had loved most in the world and certainly helped her when Anthony went to university.

"Mum where are you? I have spoken to you twice!"

Emma turned bringing herself back to the present. "Sorry Anthony, I was just thinking about the wedding and how proud I am of you. Now what did you say?"

"It's OK, nothing important. Let's get a coffee" he smiled and ushered her to the door.

Chapter 8

Leona was enthralled by Gibraltar and kept the conversation flowing with her questions and observations of the island. The coastline of Africa fascinated her and the views over the bay made her gasp with delight. The one thing she didn't like was the traffic and crowded town streets; at times it was positively hair raising trying to move about.

Fay was relieved that Leona was so interested in her surroundings. It meant she wasn't having to think too much, and it helped keep her mind off Thomas.

"Let's have coffee before we start, Leona. The café behind the museum is lovely and tranquil." And I can take something for my headache, she thought.

"That would be lovely." Leona smiled and turned her attention back to the views. Fay was certainly not planning to talk about herself but even though they had only spent a short time together, Leona had taken a liking to her.

The café was in a perfect little courtyard with tiny tables dotted around, a haven from the crowded shopping area and the noisy streets. It was very quaint and English, although around the garden items were on show which made customers aware that they were in a foreign land with an exotic history.

"Why did you come to Gibraltar, Fay?" Leona asked and then as she watched the change in Fay's expression, she knew she had asked the wrong question.

"Sorry, I'm not prying, it was just a casual question, I didn't mean to offend." She felt they had developed a good rapport and didn't want to frighten Fay off by being too inquisitive.

Fay composed herself. "It's OK Leona, I don't think you are being nosy at all. I decided to change the direction that my life was heading, and saw Emma's advert. I contacted the agency for details. It seemed to fit the bill so I applied and the rest, as they say, is history."

The waiter arrived with their drinks, giving them both a few minutes to think before saying anything else.

As they sipped their coffee and exchanged pleasantries Fay scolded herself. 'I must not be so jumpy, Leona could not know about Thomas and after all these years I should stop feeling guilty; after all, she hadn't known she was the 'other woman'.

"It's really lovely here Fay. I am so glad you were able to come shopping with me. I would like to get something for Emma, not the usual flowers but something that will always remind her of our wedding day."

"Well in that case we had better drink our coffee and shop," Fay smiled.

The next hour passed with general chatter in between shops and gradually they realised there was a lot of common ground between them. They found a bench near a small park and sat down to look at the beautiful shawl that Leona had bought for Emma.

Leona had not asked her any more direct questions about her past but Fay realised that she had said more about it to Leona than she had to anyone else. Leona was easy to talk to, but still she felt somewhat uneasy about how easily Leona got her to talk about herself.

"Well, now I think it is time we got down to some serious shopping, Leona. What do you still need?"

Leona searched her bag for her list.

"An outfit for the evening. Nothing seemed right at home."

She found the slip of paper and put it on the table to tick off a few things.

"Oh don't look so worried, I know I am hopeless but I'm sure you will work magic for me."

"I think you have too much faith in me. Although, I do know some good places to start with and if you don't like anything there we can pop over to Spain tomorrow. There is a little boutique I sometimes use which might have something suitable."

They picked up their bags and walked back to the busy shopping area, both now entirely committed to their shopping expedition.

Nathan had risen early despite being late to bed. He had only managed four hours sleep but he was used to long days and short nights. He'd enjoyed the evening, much to his surprise. Anthony and Leona were always good company and easy to be with; he could relax with them and he had not expected to find Emma and Fay such good company.

He didn't socialise a lot, and when his wife died he'd shut himself off from his friends in an attempt to deal with his grief, and had become a bit of a loner. Anthony had helped him get back into things again.

He'd never asked any questions about his family, although over time Nathan had told him about his loss. Anthony accepted that Nathan's job meant his hours were flexible and he could be away for long periods of time. Nathan didn't want to lie to him, so said he worked for the government. Anthony had accepted this, although on one occasion he had probed a little more.

Nathan just said that as he was a civil servant he couldn't discuss his work. Anthony never asked him about work again. An invisible line had been drawn and neither of them stepped over that line. Work was a subject they never discussed.

He pulled his mind back to the note which had been slipped under his door during the night. He heard the noise and yet there was no one in the corridor when he checked. Whoever left it was obviously familiar with the layout of the hotel or very quick on their feet.

The note was to let him know that one of the suspects had arrived in Gibraltar and a description would follow shortly. There didn't appear to have been any contact with the dealers they were keeping under surveillance.

He read it again, this time memorizing its contents and the style of writing. Then he burnt it in an ashtray. After washing the ashtray he went out on the balcony, his mind going off on a complete tangent as he looked out over the Island, and wondering what the last night's fuss in the car park was about.

He had decided it was not a good idea to let Fay walk out to the car even though she seemed fine about it, so he turned and went after her. As he reached the entrance he saw her near a car with the door half open. He'd assumed it was hers. She seemed to be arguing with someone. He thought it was a man but the car park was not well lit so he could not be sure exactly who. Perhaps a boyfriend, annoyed that he had not been invited tonight? At one point it appeared things got a bit heated but before he could interfere, Fay got into the car and drove off at speed, leaving tyre tracks behind her. It was over in minutes. He waited until the other person left to make sure she wasn't followed before he returned to the casino.

Odd, but none of my business, he thought, although he'd been able to confirm it was a man talking to Fay. He had seen him as he stepped out of the shadows when Fay drove away.

Oh well, it's nothing to do with me if her boyfriend was angry. He turned his mind back to his investigation but couldn't deny feeling some concern for Fay's safety.

The squad had received information from a reliable source that there was a shipment of drugs and possibly weapons being sent via Gibraltar for distribution in Europe. Detailed plans were not available yet but the informant was hoping to provide more information asap. Nathan had been asked to get in touch with the local contact and ferret around. He was to assist customs as and when requested but take a lead for the drug squad on the island. His identity was only known by a few officers. This anonymity was a real plus as everyone seemed to know everyone else on the island.

Walking out onto his balcony he opened the map he'd been given and studied it, looking for both obvious and less obvious routes that this shipment could arrive.

Obvious routes were boat or by vehicle through the border but both seemed risky. Vehicles were checked randomly all the time and the coast guard maintained records of vessels arriving or departing. Perhaps a parachute drop, but this seemed unlikely as the plane could be easily spotted.

After about 40 minutes of trying to familiarize himself with the map he decided to take a walk over to Spain to see just how tight the security was. He walked back into his room and looked at the clock. It was later than he thought. 'Damn!', he thought, 'I was supposed to meet Anthony 15 minutes ago.' Putting the papers back into the case he locked them in the room safe. His walk into Spain would have to wait.

Grabbing his jacket, he flicked it over his shoulder and feeling a thud, he remembered his gun. Normally he would not carry a weapon; he hated guns or knives, all too often he saw the results of them being used. On this job his head of department had insisted he must be armed.

All personnel working in the drug squads had weapons training and he, along with most of his colleagues, hated carrying them and avoided using them unless the situation demanded it. Using force to defeat force didn't make sense to him or his colleagues but sometimes there was no option.

Emma and Anthony were preparing drinks when Nathan arrived. They were discussing the previous evening and Emma was boasting about her win and asking Anthony for details of the wedding.

"The dress is exquisite, Anthony. You are a lucky man." She smiled, not giving him any further information.

Nathan apologised for being late. As he sipped his drink Emma suggested they give him a tour of the island. Perfect he thought, I can look around whilst appearing to be sightseeing. Although he did feel that he was abusing Emma's friendship, the opportunity was too good to miss.

"Sorry Mum but I have to check in with work and meet the girls, so I will give the tour a miss." Anthony finished his drink.

"Right, I will leave you in my mother's capable hands, Nathan. Bye Mum, see you both later."

As he drove off, Emma asked Nathan if there was any particular part of the island he was interested in, or was he happy with a general tour?

"A general tour will be fine Emma," he smiled. "It's kind of you to give up your time. At some time I would like to walk over to Spain, just to say I've done it."

"A sightseeing tour it is then." Emma smiled as she picked up her car keys and ushered him out of the door.

Chapter 9

They started by going to the highest part of the island, looking out over the sea towards Morocco and down onto the old water catchments. It was a lovely day and the views were spectacular. As the sun touched the blue sea it sparkled and made him blink it was so bright.

In the heat haze Morocco looked mysterious and inviting. Next they visited the apes. Nathan enjoyed seeing them run free but was careful not to get too close. He'd noticed one or two of them were really cheeky and pestered people to give them food and got annoyed if they didn't get something. One snatched a handbag off a tourist because she didn't feed him.

Emma suggested they drive around the island and then perhaps see the caves. He couldn't believe his luck. This meant he would have covered some of the sites he wanted to check out, which would save him time. He had intended to contact the local police chief to find out how they thought the drugs were being smuggled in, and to ask about the caves. Then the note he had received advised him not to contact anyone, not even the police, indicating that this could compromise his cover.

Looking at Emma just for a second, it crossed his mind that she could be his contact, but no, she was not the type. He hated not knowing who he was dealing with; still time would tell.

When they had covered the coastline they drove up to the caves. They were very impressive and he was surprised how big they were. There was a cavern that was used for concerts, and he could imagine the acoustics would be incredible. Then they went on to the fortified caves where there was a small exhibition.

Although this was a little touristy for him, it was still of interest. Slowly the chill in the caves began to make them both feel cold, and they headed out again into the sunshine.

Nathan asked Emma if she would book tickets for one of the concerts. He felt sure it would be an experience not to be missed. Although he was trying to conceal his interest he had been making a careful mental note of the caves and as they came out he tried to look around the surrounding area without being too obvious.

"Well I don't know about you, Nathan, but I would like some lunch. I know a nice little bistro part-way down to the town. Shall we?" Emma asked.

"I think that is a great idea, let's go." He suddenly realised he was quite hungry.

"Maybe we will bump into the others."

The bistro was quiet and they had no problem getting a table and chose to sit by the door. The waiter bought over the drinks, then as the he walked away, Nathan noticed some sort of disturbance in the corner.

A waiter was arguing with a man. Looking around the restaurant the waiter seemed to realise they were attracting attention. The conversation ended abruptly, one of the men walked past them brushing the table as he went out into the street.

He looked familiar but Nathan couldn't remember where he had seen him before. There was something about him but hard as he tried, Nathan couldn't recall where he had seen him. The waiter watched the man walk away then glanced across at Nathan and Emma before he went into the kitchen.

It was obvious to everyone in the bistro that there had been an altercation between the two men. No one could have failed to notice the look of annoyance on the man's face as he walked out of the bistro. Emma didn't acknowledge him in any way, which was odd, as she seemed to know everyone on the island. If he knew the waiter, surely he would have known Emma. Probably not a resident then.

"I hope you enjoyed the tour, Nathan?"

He realised Emma had been talking to him.

"Sorry Emma, I was thinking about the concert in the caves; I have thoroughly enjoyed the tour thank you."

The waiter arrived with their food, but whilst chatting to Emma as they ate their meal his mind kept working.

That was it! The man had reminded him of the one in the casino car park.

If he was the same man how did he know Fay? Nathan frowned, perhaps I should take a closer look into her past. Anthony and Emma had said little about Fay since they had arrived.

Putting his thoughts on hold till he could think things through in more depth, he smiled at Emma.

"This food is excellent."

Emma had been watching Nathan closely. He couldn't have failed to notice the two men arguing. Pity they hadn't been nearer then she could have heard the conversation. She didn't recognise the man who'd rudely pushed past them as he left the bistro.

Not local, perhaps a tourist who hadn't enjoyed his meal. She did, however, know the waiter. He was from a local family who were always in trouble, never anything serious, just petty theft, drunkenness and that kind of thing.

Having finished their lunch it was time to continue the tour. Emma pushed the incident to the back of her mind, it was probably a dispute over the bill.

Turning to Nathan she asked if he wanted to carry on with the tour.

"If you don't mind, Emma, I would like to take a walk. The tropical gardens we walked through to the casino looked interesting, and it would be nice to see them by day".

The gardens were at the back of the hotel so it made sense to walk back up the hill to take a look. The car, parked in the bistro lay-by would be fine for an hour or so.

Nathan felt uneasy, wanting to get to work as quickly as he could and didn't want to be wasting so much time 'sightseeing'. Then again, this tour was helping him find the lay of the land. He wished he knew the identity of his contact but his briefing had made it clear that they should not meet unless the job unexpectedly took off.

Emma was telling him the names of the plants in the garden and then seemed to realise that he was not really interested. She smiled to herself, typical man, Frank could never tell one plant from another.

"This path leads to the harbour. If you'd like to walk down." She smiled. It was obvious his mind was elsewhere. "It shouldn't take a youngster like you long, I'll go back for the car."

"A walk would be great, if are your sure you don't mind me deserting you, Emma. I'd still like to cross the border into Spain so I might carry on and do it now."

"Of course not, we'll catch up later. Enjoy the walk," she said strolling off in the direction of the car.

Nathan continued walking down through the gardens following the path and eventually arriving at the waterfront. He slowed his pace a little as he continued to the harbour. Now he was on his own, his mind returned to the two men in the bistro and the possibility of a connection to Fay. He looked out over the blue sparkling sea and let his mind work, whilst noting the various small craft bobbing about on the gentle swell.

If only I had overheard some of their argument, he frowned, hoping Fay wasn't involved with the stranger. He'd looked like he could be trouble.

Walking along the wharf he kept trying to remember anything that would prove a connection but from the little information he had about Fay, there didn't seem to be one.

He had begun to take interest in the moored yachts. There was certainly some money tied up here. Smaller vessels were moored alongside the more expensive ones creating a haphazard collage along the pontoons. Several ocean-going yachts were moored together alongside the larger jetty by the clubhouse. He sat on the wall and noticed there was a flurry of activity on one of the large vessels. The crew on deck were very busy, smart uniforms, he thought.

Suddenly he heard raised voices which became louder until it was obvious that someone was in trouble. Looking to see who was making all the noise he recognized the man from the bistro. He appeared to be getting a good ticking off and things were getting more heated by the minute. It appeared he was having difficulty understanding his colleague. Well that could answer one question, he probably wasn't local.

Still, he was someone worth checking out. Customs should have some information on him. A visit to the Harbour Master might be in order, as he wanted more details on some of the yachts and owners anyway.

The larger vessels were of special interest. Looking along the moored yachts, Nathan noted vessel names and port of registration. Drugs and arms smuggled in by private yacht, why not? The fact it was so obvious that to some extent made it less risky.

All vessels coming into the harbour were inspected by customs. Would it be possible to put someone ashore without customs spotting them? Perhaps the drugs were dropped overboard whilst at sea, weighed down for collection later. There would be many hiding places on board and it would not be easy to search every inch of the bigger yachts. Some seemingly inaccessible places were bound to be missed. There was always the possibility of bribery. Personal gain was generally a factor in any crime.

Expensive yachts, rich people, and drugs would be a lucrative way of funding the lifestyle they were used to, or wanted to get used to. He needed to get information on these vessels as soon as he could, the 'Flight of Freedom' especially, as it was the vessel the man he wished to identify was on.

The island was small so anything unusual would be noticed, which meant a resident would be invaluable in helping the smugglers. If this operation turned out to be genuine then someone who lived on the island could well be involved. The image of Fay and the man outside the casino came to mind, and he wished he'd got a better look at him. Still, an identity check may confirm his suspicions.

Getting to his feet he continued walking along the waterfront towards the town. Could she be involved? He couldn't see it somehow, but some people got away with crime by appearing innocent and respectable. This idea settled in the back of his mind and kept coming back to annoy him. As he got near the town he searched his memory again, trying to recall every detail Emma or Anthony had mentioned about Fay. In truth, it was very little.

I'll contact H.Q. and ask for an urgent background check on Fay; there was always the possibility her life here was a cover story. It wouldn't be the first time he had found someone seemingly respectable to be heavily involved in criminal activities.

Chapter 10

Emma arrived home to find her son waiting for her.

"What happened to lunch with the girls?"

"We had lunch then I was politely requested to go away, so I came back here to see my old mum."

Emma playfully punched him.

"Leona is enchanting, I'm sure she would not tell you to go away. I think she will be a delightful daughter-in-law. You haven't told me much about her, has she family, what sort of work does she do?"

"Well as it is me, your son, she is marrying how could she be anything else? Would I choose anyone less than perfect?"

Leaning forward he put his arm around Emma.

"You always talk as if your time with Dad was perfect and I want the same for us." Skilfully, Anthony had avoided answering his mother's questions.

"Conceited oaf." Emma replied, but a shadow crossed her face.

Frank would be so proud of Anthony. It was times like this she missed him and wondered what their lives would have been like if he was still alive. Would Angel have grown into the daughter she hoped for and gone to college or married and have children of her own by now? She sighed, no good going down that route.

It had been hard coping on her own bringing up her son but Anthony had been so good, never giving her cause to worry. He had gone through the usual problems of youth but had never got into any real trouble. When he had chosen to go to university in England she had been devastated, but knew that his decision was sensible.

He always joked that she packed him off to England when all he wanted was to bum around Gibraltar, but she knew he was restless and felt restricted living on the island. Emma pulled her thoughts back to the present.

"What does Nathan do for a living, Anthony? You've never said. He is certainly going to be popular with the females of the island."

Anthony had seen the look on his mother's face and knew she was thinking about his father and the sister he would never know. It was difficult for him, but he empathized with her sense of loss. For him there was only a feeling of sadness that he would never have the chance to meet them.

"He's a civil servant, quite high up I believe. As to his romantic involvements, he was married but she died and that is all I am going to say, mother. He likes to keep things locked up inside and I value his friendship too much to pry."

He sipped his tea smiling at her impatience.

"Seriously, I would rather not talk about Nathan. Suffice it to say he has known great loss and sadness and he is a very special friend to me and that is all I need to know about him."

"Just like your father, judge by deeds not hearsay. The inner man is what matters, not the outer shell." She leaned forward and refilled their cups.

"Sad though, how people suffer and may never find happiness and peace again. He seems too nice to spend his life alone."

"Well moving on, what is Fay's story? It's clear you are very fond of her."

Emma put her cup down and took a moment to answer.

"When I first met Fay she struck me as fragile, like a piece of Dresden, a little chipped and in need of care. You're right, I am extremely fond of her. It seems she is alone in this world, at least no one has contacted her since she worked for me. Like Nathan, she doesn't like to discuss her past and I know she would resent me prying."

She leaned forward and tapped his arm. "Another one of life's lonely, crushed people. Now let's get down to business and ensure this wedding goes without a hitch."

Anthony was as disappointed as his mother had been when he declined to discuss Nathan. He'd hoped his mother would give him a bit more information on Fay.

She seemed very fond of Fay, and he wanted to be sure his mother's trust was not being abused.

"I can't be responsible for discussing details with you unless Leona is here. Let's wait till we are all together." Smiling, he put his arm round her. "There is plenty of time Mum."

Chapter 11

Fay and Leona shopped till they couldn't shop any more. Finally exhausted they went to the hotel and ordered tea. As they drove past the casino, Fay's mind went back to the previous night. She thought she had seen Thomas several times in the town and then realised it was someone else.

'Stop it', she told herself, 'you are just rattled', but her thoughts kept returning to him. Time had been good to him. He was still handsome; even in her shocked state she had registered that he was still as attractive as when they first met. Why had he come back, her life was on track now and he'd just thrown the largest spanner into the works!

They arrived at the hotel and Fay noticed the tracks she had created in her haste to get away last night. As she walked to the reception she recalled how Nathan's smile had made her feel and the intensity of emotion she had felt when they shook hands. Had she ever felt that with Thomas. 'No, stop right there!' This was somewhere she did not want to go. There could be no comparison between the two men anyway. Nathan seemed the dependable type, unlike Thomas. Fay focused her thoughts back to the present as she realised Leona was speaking to her.

"Sorry, I was thinking about last night. It was so nice wasn't it?"

Leona smiled. "That's OK, we are both a bit tired, I think. Yes, I was a little worried about meeting Emma, but thankfully she is lovely, and once that was over I relaxed and enjoyed the evening immensely."

"Do you know, Fay, I think I could enjoy being part of this family; I'm sure you know what I mean. Anthony told me how fond of you his mother is, and having met you I can see why".

"I'm hoping we will be firm friends." Leona lightly touched Fay's arm as she spoke.

"I hope so too." Tea arrived and they both sat looking at the view, lost in their own thoughts.

Why does Fay hide so much of herself, Leona thought. We have had a great time and she has asked me a lot of questions but said very little about herself. Except that she was orphaned very young and grew up with her grandparents who had both died before she was 21. They'd left her a small legacy, not a fortune but enough to make her life comfortable and secure. That's where the information stopped.

Leona sensed that someone had hurt Fay badly but could not get her to speak about any previous relationships. Perhaps the hurt is recent but whatever it is she was not going to talk to Leona about it just yet.

Fay was thinking how nice it would have been to have a close friend or sister like Leona. Her parents died in a tragic car accident when she was 8 years old. Apparently a drunk driver was to blame. The driver went to jail but to an 8-year-old that had meant nothing her parents were still dead. There were only her grandparents to take her in, which they did willingly, though in reality, they were far too old to bring up a young child. They never complained, and gave her a safe, secure life. Possibly it was a little too protected, which is why Thomas had managed to work his way into her life.

Looking back, he was probably always after her inheritance and she had not mattered to him at all. Her life was so different now, and somehow she felt that the blossoming friendship with Leona was going to be one she would treasure. She knew Emma would always be her closest friend.

Leona was immersed in her thoughts, trying to work out how she could get Fay to open up. She had not met Nathan till Anthony introduced her. He seemed nice but kept his guard up most of the time. Spending the day with Fay, she began to see similarities in Nathan's demeanour and Fay's.

Mmm… Fay and Nathan, both appearing to feel the need to protect themselves. Her mind suddenly took a different tack. Fay and Nathan? Yes, she could actually see it working. Then again she'd better not start to think along those lines. Much as she liked Fay, she wasn't here to play matchmaker.

At that moment the other half of the equation was walking into the hotel foyer.

Nathan entered the reception area and asked for his room key and as he turned he thought he heard Leona's voice. Walking across the foyer Nathan saw the girls and decided to join them.

"Hello you two, finished shopping already? By the look of those bags you've had a successful day."

They both looked round in surprise and smiled as he walked over to join them.

The waiter arrived and Nathan ordered drinks for them all.

"Did you get everything you wanted, Leona?"

"I did. Fay was a great help, she knew all the right shops and has a friend who has agreed to make my dress for the reception."

Their drinks were served and Leona took a sip from her glass.

"I bought these for Anthony, I hope he likes them. What do you think Nathan?" She handed him a tiny box.

He opened the box which contained a pair of gold cuff links each set with a heart shaped diamond. Nathan smiled and handing them back, he and Fay simultaneously said, "He will love them."

They all laughed. "Well that's unanimous then," he said, "Anthony will love them but you are the jewel in his life."

He leant forward and kissed her cheek. Blushing Leona concentrated on putting the box away, thinking 'Hmm, I wonder what they would think if they knew all this was on expenses and will have to be returned?'

Fay smiled and wondered how this man got to be so sensitive. He had seen the uncertainty in Leona's face and had responded by reassuring her in such a kind way. 'Yes, I'm warming to him.' They continued to chat whilst finishing their drinks. As expected the main topic was the wedding.

Nathan looked at this watch. "Sorry ladies, I have to go. Can I get you another drink first?"

They both declined and went back to their shopping and wedding talk and seemed engrossed when he looked back.

They sat chatting for a while then Fay suddenly found herself issuing an invitation to Leona for everyone to come to her for supper.

"I've only got a small house so I don't entertain very often. It would make a nice change. Do you think you could arrange things with the others, Leona?"

"I would really like that. We'll give Nathan a ring from reception, I can check with Emma and Anthony when you drop me off, which I think should be soon or the bridegroom may think we have got lost."

They rang Nathan and then collected the packages and walked out to the car.

"Don't you think Nathan is good looking, Fay?" Leona watched Fay's reaction to her question, attempting to gauge if Fay already had a man on the scene.

"I hadn't thought about it," she lied hoping that she had not shown how much he unnerved her. "Now you mention it I suppose he is quite attractive. He seems a sensitive person and kind which is nice."

They reached the car. "Let's get these parcels stowed and get you back."

Leona smiled and dropped the subject as they drove along, her mind in overdrive.

So it didn't appear that Fay was involved with anyone, which was odd, as she was not only good looking but was pleasant to be with. Strange someone hadn't snapped her up yet.

Fay was trying to decide if Leona was matchmaking, trying to find out if she thought Nathan was attractive. Surely not, after all she hardly knew Fay. Well, Leona would be disappointed, I am not in the mood for any romantic involvements at the moment.

She'd been pretty shocked at seeing Thomas again and regardless of her reaction to Nathan she was not in the frame of mind to consider getting involved with anyone.

"Right Leona, see you about 7.30, don't expect too much. I am a very basic cook."

Fay smiled as she drove away. Fortunate I made that huge lasagne this morning. That won't be going in the freezer now. Dessert and starter were easy so there was not a lot of work for her to do. Just need to collect some salad and cream on the way home, she thought. Main thing will be to tidy round as I left in such a hurry this morning.

Chapter 12

Fay had showered, her make-up and hair were done. Plenty of time, I think I'll go down and sort everything before I get dressed, just in case I spill something on my clothes. She was putting the finishing touch to the table when her doorbell rang.

Frowning she considered ignoring it but then thought maybe Emma has come to help out. As she opened the door and saw him standing there she hesitated for a second and then pushed the door, intending to shut it but he was too quick, his foot was in the reveal before she could close it. Still she tried to push it shut hoping he would be forced to remove his foot.

"Oh, come on Fay, let me in, we have things to say to each other." Thomas was pushing against the door trying to force his way in.

"We have nothing to say to each other, I hoped you had got the message and left." She tried again to push the door against him. "Go away and stay away." As she said these words he seemed to release his pressure on the door but then he gave one huge push which threw her off balance. She felt her head spin as she fell back and hit the wall, knocking the hall table over as she fell. Her mind registered the sound of things falling onto the tiled floor.

Fay tried to regain her balance but Thomas was standing close, hovering over her making it difficult for her to move.

"You look as lovely as ever. I'm sorry if I hurt you but I wanted to explain that I am free now. I have never stopped loving you. Won't you give me another chance, Fay?"

His words seemed to give her the strength to shout out her reply.

"No!" She spat the word out. Forcing your way in here proves you haven't changed. I am expecting company, so please go and don't come back."

She tried to straighten up again but he was too close. She didn't have room to move and could only remain in a semi-crouched position. Her head was hurting, she felt dizzy and nauseous.

Thomas bent closer to her, and frightened, she tried to push him away with her arm. He seemed surprised by her attempt to fend him off and stepped back. Fay took the chance to move towards the lounge, still crouching as she slid across the tiled floor.

Her mind was in turmoil. What did he want, and why had he not left when she told him to go? Fear was raging through her. She felt the cold ceramic tiles on her body and remembered that she was not fully dressed. Realising that he was now between her and the front door effectively blocking her escape, she tried again to stand up but he was too quick.

Grabbing her around her waist, half lifting her, he pushed her into the lounge and pinned her against the wall. Her head banged against the wall with the force he used.

Everything seemed to go dark, her head was full of pain and bright lights then she felt herself slipping down to the floor. Thomas released his grip slightly letting her fall but still imprisoning her against the wall. In that split second she realised that she had to get away.

Fight back, her mind seemed to shout, don't let him win. Frantically she started struggling, trying desperately to free herself. He was too strong and laughed at her attempts escape. Eventually managing to grab her arms, Thomas pushed them back trapping them behind her. Pain seared through her shoulders.

"You know we have unfinished business Fay," he whispered in her ear, "If you won't listen to me then today is the day we settle that business." Lifting her slightly, he viciously twisted her body, pulling her closer to him. She tried to free her arms, he pushed her harder against the wall increasing his grip causing her to cry out in pain.

She realised she was crying as she begged him to release her but Thomas just smiled and then started to kiss her, forcing his tongue between her lips. Fear shot through her as she realised he was trying to pull her robe off.

'He's going to rape me!' As the thought sprang into her head the realisation of his intentions caused panic to take over.

Fight, fight! The word kept going round and round in her head. Her arms were still trapped, she could only kick out with one leg. It was useless. She was pleading with him now to let her go, trying somehow to get through to him but he ignored her words.

Thomas had freed her gown and was pressing hard against her. He slid his hand roughly down her body. Slowly he stroked her breast and pinched her nipple so hard she cried out. He laughed and then sliding his hand further down he pushed his hand between her legs. Fay was begging him to let her go. As he started pulling at her underwear she heard him laugh and then felt the burning pain on her thigh as the elastic cut into her skin. Still she struggled in a desperate effort to free herself. Her arms now filled with excruciating pain as he pressed his body hard against her. Thomas's hot breath seemed to fill her ear then he started kissing her neck. Hard, biting kisses meant to bruise and cause her pain.

Fear and panic were slowly being replaced by resignation, she couldn't see any way to stop him. He had managed to get a grip on her knickers and was tearing at them. The flimsy material was no resistance for him, she felt the elastic score her skin as they were torn apart.

He started to run his hand across her abdomen. Fay still struggled to free herself but felt the fight leaving her as he became more excited and forceful. In his excitement he pushed her even harder into the wall behind her. She thought her arms would break with the force. He took no notice of her pain or tears in fact she felt he enjoyed hearing her plead with him to stop.

She lost any hope that he would free her, knowing she couldn't take any more, it was futile. She didn't have the strength left to fight him. He is going to rape me and I cannot do anything to stop him.

Suddenly she was free.

Slumped back against the wall, her arms free but so painful, she couldn't move them.

What's happening? Something had made him stop; it didn't matter, she was free. Her mind said run, get away from him but her legs wouldn't respond. Slowly she slid down the wall falling in a heap onto the cold tiles.

Sounds began to reach through her panic-stricken mind. Shouting and scuffling noises. Was that a car door, an engine? Too frightened and exhausted to move she listened, praying Thomas had left. Then there were skidding sounds, a car driving off in a hurry.

Thank goodness! He had seen sense changed his mind. He was driving away. Fay glanced quickly round the room, trying to make certain Thomas wasn't there. He wasn't, he'd really gone. She shivered and reached for the shreds of her gown, pulled it across the floor and tried to wrap it around herself.

She knew her legs wouldn't hold her, so she began to crawl towards a chair. Then she heard a sound which sent a chill through her.

'Footsteps, she heard footsteps!'

'Please no, please don't come back.'

Silently she pleaded with Thomas as tears slid down her cheeks. Shaking but unable to move, fear began to take hold again. She waited unable to fight any more unable to run away.

Then someone said, "It's OK. He's gone."

Then he was trying to wrap something round her. In panic, she struggled to get free.

It wasn't Thomas. The man's voice was gentle, trying to reassure her, telling her she was safe. He managed to lift her from the floor, holding her firmly he carried her to a chair, whilst she continued struggling, desperate to get free.

She didn't want to be touched she wanted to be left alone.

Nathan sat next to Fay, reassuring her over and over, telling her she was safe, soothing her as best he could. He asked if she was hurt, did she want a doctor? Fay didn't speak. She stopped struggling as she began to realise it was not Thomas holding her. Eventually she began to sob, heart rending sobs.

Nathan's anger grew as she cried and uttered unintelligible words. He wished he'd had more time with the man he'd found assaulting her. He would have given him the thrashing he deserved.

"It's Nathan, Fay, you are safe now. He's gone and won't be back to hurt you. Please tell me do you need a doctor?"

She just kept sobbing, uttering occasional words which made no sense to him. Emma was mentioned, someone called Thomas and several times she asked, 'why?'

Eventually she seemed to calm a little and his voice at last registered. She shook her head in answer to his question.

"Nathan? How?" She tried to understand what had happened. "You saved me, I couldn't stop him, I tried but he was too strong." Tears flowed across her cheeks as she spoke.

"Come on, I'm going to take you upstairs. Fay please, I just don't think you can manage without help." He explained quickly as he felt her stiffen. "Then I will call the police."

"No, please don't call them, I don't want anyone else to know about this." Fay whispered, panic evident in her words.

"OK. If that's how you want it, but are you sure you are not hurt?" Nathan wasn't convinced she didn't need a doctor.

"Yes, all I want is a shower. I feel bruised and dirty. I want to wash the smell and touch of Thomas from my skin." She stood up shakily.

Then seeing the hall table which had been turned over in the struggle, and the phone on the floor, her brain clicked into gear.

"Oh no! What about the others!"

"It's OK, I'll call them, say you are unwell and I will stay down here if you want me to. Then you can be sure he doesn't come back." Nathan smiled reassuringly. "Go on up and have a shower and when you are ready call me and I will make you a drink." Gently he put his hands on her shoulders and pointed her towards the stairs.

He watched Fay as she climbed the stairs and waited till he heard the shower running. Then he picked up the table and phone. Whilst he waited for Fay to finish her shower he thought over what she had said. Thomas, so that was his name and Fay obviously did know him. What was this all about? His mind was full of questions.

He reached for the phone, relieved when he heard the dialling tone, he pulled out his diary and found Emma's number.

"Emma, it's Nathan. I'm at Fay's, yes. Unfortunately she's not feeling well so tonight is cancelled. Would you let Anthony know? What? No, it's only a migraine, all she wants is her bed and some painkillers. I'll make sure she has everything she needs before I leave. See you tomorrow then, Bye." He rang off before Emma could ask any more questions.

Putting the phone back on the cradle he listened, the shower was still running. Walking back into the lounge his mind began to ramble.

Chapter 13

It was sheer good fortune he'd been there. He was driving a hire car back to the hotel when he realised he would be passing Fay's door. Checking the time, he thought it was silly going back to the hotel, and he didn't think Fay would mind if he was early. It gave him the opportunity to find out a little more about her.

He'd seen a car parked near her house and almost drove off, then thought he heard raised voices. Deciding to make sure everything was OK, he got out of the car he walked towards the house. When he got nearer he realised that the door was open, then he heard Fay's voice pleading with someone to let her go. As he stepped through the door he saw a man pinning Fay to the wall.

Grabbing the man, he pulled him away. He was struggling with him when he heard Fay cry out and he lost his concentration. The man took his opportunity and made his escape. Nathan's immediate instinct was to chase after him but Fay's distraught cry made him go to her instead. He didn't want to think what could have happened if he had driven off thinking Fay had company when he saw a car outside her house.

Fay would be pleased that he had stopped Emma coming over, but he wasn't happy to leave her alone tonight. Maybe it would be an idea if he stayed. He was still not sure she hadn't been hurt. If I had been a few minutes later... anger started to course through him.

I wish I'd been able to stop him escaping, then I would have made sure he wasn't going to come back. Lost in his thoughts he hadn't noticed the shower had stopped. Opening the cupboard doors he eventually found some paracetamol. He made some coffee and then poured a large glass of brandy. Placing everything on a tray he went upstairs, pausing on the landing he listened. Standing still, he waited trying to work out which door he should go to, then the sound of Fay's quiet sobs reached him. Gently he tapped the door.

"Fay, it's Nathan. I've made a drink for you. Shall I leave it here or can I come in with it?" No reply.

"Look I just want to make sure you are OK, then I will leave you in peace." After a few seconds the door opened.

"I'm fine, really, I don't want to imagine what would have happened if you had not arrived but I would like to go to bed now, I feel so drained I can't think straight."

She looked so helpless, so defenceless. Nathan wanted to reach out and hold her, reassure her, instinct told him she wouldn't want anyone near her.

"Here," he offered her the tray. "I think this will help, if you are sure you don't need a doctor or the police, then take some pills and try to sleep. I'll just tidy up a bit downstairs and then lock up." She nodded, took the tray and shut the door without uttering another word.

Staring at the closed door he felt such anger against the man that had done this to her. 'There is no way I'm leaving her on her own tonight.' He walked down the stairs and started clearing up. The sofa looked comfy and he didn't think she would come down till the morning, by which time he would be gone. He was used to night vigils and early departures.

Nathan walked to the front door, opened and shut it noisily, then turned the key as quietly as he could. Walking back into the lounge and picking up the throw he had tried to wrap round Fay earlier, he settled down on the sofa for the night. Just in case that creep came back or she was hurt and didn't want to tell him.

He'd been so angry when he saw Fay being attacked, all sense of reason went out of the window. During the night he was kept awake by the realisation that Fay had somehow got under his skin. 'This is work, and she could be part of the gang I am after,' he reminded himself. In his heart he knew Fay's was an issue that would have to be dealt with sooner rather than later. In the back of his mind the question of her involvement in the case was still niggling away.

Nathan shut the door quietly, turned the key in the lock and slipped it through the letter box. Before he left, he'd listened outside Fay's bedroom door but there was no sound.

Hoping that she was asleep he left a note with his mobile number saying she could ring if she needed him, promising to call her later. It was only 6.30 am. too early to disturb her if she was asleep and hopefully she was.

He slipped the car into gear and took off the handbrake, not starting the engine till he had rolled down the road a little way. He didn't want to wake Fay if she was sleeping.

As the engine sparked into life he went over the events of the previous evening again. Seeing Fay looking so thoroughly defeated last night had affected him more than he cared to admit. A small dent had been made in his emotional shield. He shook his head reminding himself that now was not the time to let the wall around his heart drop.

Jumbled thoughts had kept him awake most of the night. It was around 5 am when he decided that the man he had seen in the casino car park was the same man he'd seen at the bistro and on the yacht. He obviously had some sort of connection with her, perhaps he was an ex-boyfriend. He recalled Emma telling him Fay had no relatives, then again, she could have lied to Emma. She had tried to tell him who Thomas was, but he had stopped her, not wanting her to become even more distressed. Now he wished he had listened to her then, at least he might have a better idea of how she was connected to this man. Whoever he was, he was a nasty piece of work and needed investigating, which Nathan would arrange asap.

After a shower and shave he decided to take a walk down to the harbour and look around, perhaps have a quiet word with the harbour officials about that yacht. He'd intended to do it yesterday but changed his mind, now he wished he'd had not waited. If he could find out who the owner the vessel was and get a list of the crew's names, he could get them checked out quickly. He would be closer to finding out what the connection was between Fay and Thomas.

Just for a second he recalled Fay's shattered look when she opened the bedroom door the previous night. He really hoped she was not mixed up in something dodgy, she didn't seem the type. Then again, past experience had proved there was no type. Money, excitement of the danger and occasionally just circumstances were generally at the root of crime.

Chapter 14

By now he was sure Emma would have been in touch with Fay, so he would leave it till later to call and check on her. Picking up his coat he looked round the room, already concentrating on his visit to the harbour. As he stepped out of the lift the receptionist called him.

"Good morning sir, I have just rung your room. A message was left for you last night."

The receptionist pulled an envelope from the post rack. "Here it is." smiling she handed Nathan the envelope. "Have a good day, sir."

He put the letter in his pocket and walked out of the hotel towards the tropical gardens, found a seat and sat down to read the letter. No clues of its origin from the envelope or the message inside. The was only a sheet of paper from his contact, giving a map reference and a time, and suggesting they meet the next day. He presumed that the map required was of the island as nothing else had been stated. So the planned trip across the border into Spain would have to be postponed.

Tearing the letter into tiny pieces he placed some in each of his pockets, intending to burn them later in the hotel. The map reference and time were already memorised.

It crossed his mind to question the validity of the letter, it could be a trap. Shrugging his shoulders, he decided that whatever, the appointment had to kept. Standing up he looked around but could not see anyone else in the garden, so resumed his walk to the harbour.

Nathan's thoughts were mainly focused on the yachts and the visit to the customs office. He had been loath to appear in person as his cover could be compromised but something was niggling away at him and the customs office was the only place where he might find some answers.

As he looked out over the harbour, squinting in the glare of the sun on the blue ocean, his mind began to ramble. He should check on Fay as soon as he could. She may be a suspect but even so she had been badly scared last night. Whilst he didn't think her attacker would return so soon, she would be feeling pretty rotten today.

Fay had slept surprisingly well, but within seconds of waking, the previous night's events flooded her mind. Her body was aching and when she looked at her arms and legs there were several bruises appearing. The weal across her abdomen was sore and red where Thomas had torn her panties. There was bruising beginning to show on her face. Sighing, Fay sat up to get out of bed but the muscles in her arms felt weak and didn't seem to want to support her.

Gingerly she slid her legs of the bed and stepped into her slippers, walked over to the dressing table dreading what she would see, and on seeing her reflection she started to cry. Her eyes were red and swollen and the corner of her lip was bruised, there were signs of bruising on her cheeks and her neck. How on earth am I going to pass this off, she thought, then remembering Nathan had already seen her she realised it would be impossible to pretend to anyone that nothing was wrong.

Tears threatened again as she recalled his kindness, but could she be sure he wouldn't tell anyone about what had happened? A deep sense of embarrassment and shame crept over her as she recalled how he'd helped her. When he had first come to her aid she'd fought him, feeling vulnerable, frightened and not knowing who it was holding her. Gradually he had calmed her, holding her whilst she sobbed. When he had suggested carrying her to the bedroom she panicked, but he'd understood, leaving her to deal with her emotions in her own way.

In between sobs she had tried to explain what had happened, who Thomas was, but Nathan stopped her, saying there was no need to explain anything. What must he think of her. How could she face him again?

This morning she felt dirty, worthless and couldn't understand why Thomas had tried to rape her. He'd seemed so full of anger and hatred towards her. Why had she not checked before opening the door, or at least got dressed? It was her fault, all her fault. She should never have opened the door when she was not fully dressed.

When Nathan knocked on her bedroom door last night, she had ignored the knocking, unable to face him knowing that he had witnessed some of the attack. Now she felt a rush of embarrassment, surely he'd have seen her half-naked when he had wrapped her in the throw. It was the gentleness of his voice which in the end made her open the bedroom door. He had only wanted to check she was OK and give her a drink and some pills.

Would he tell Emma? Panic coursed through her. How can I face anyone, especially Emma? Nathan would surely think it was my fault. How could he know that Thomas was not her boyfriend, but a nightmare from her past?

The sound of the phone ringing shattered the uneasy silence. Ignoring it, Fay went upstairs to have another shower, hoping that somehow it would wash away the memory of Thomas's hands on her body.

At first the warmth of the water seemed to soothe her bruised skin, then she began to scrub her body vigorously till her skin felt sore. Exhausted she leant against the tiles, slowly sliding down the wall, curling up beneath the hot water, sobbing as the water washed over her.

Chapter 15

Thomas looked in the mirror, his eye hurt and now he could see why, it was already turning red from the punch that bloke had thrown. Oh well, in his circles that was normal, in fact it was almost a badge of honour. There would be a few ribald comments but no one would pry. He hadn't seen the bloke coming, he'd been too busy taking his revenge on Fay. Suddenly someone was pulling him away from her, there was a brief struggle then the stranger thumped him. In his hurry to get away he didn't stop to look who had hit him.

Stupid really, he should have left things alone, especially with the job about to take off. He'd seen Fay go into her house the previous day when he left the bistro; she looked great.

Memories surfaced and for some stupid reason he decided to call on her. It was her refusal to talk to him that had made him angry. None of his girlfriends had kept him dangling like she had. He paid a dear price for her morals. He'd felt it was time for her to pay, after all the trouble she had caused him.

Because of her, Debra had taken him to the cleaners, ruined his life and landed him in prison for bigamy. Fay wasn't his first affair, but for some reason this time Debra had delved into his past. She was more than happy to find he was already married and that he had two other children. Talk about a woman scorned, she wanted revenge and went all out to get it. His legal wife was only too pleased to help her and finally see the back of him.

His name had been plastered all over the papers. Of course, he was sent down and when he was released couldn't get work. He needed to get away. Nobody was going to help him after the character assassination Debra had so carefully and completely orchestrated. He blamed Fay totally, the stupid bitch had spoilt everything. If she had played ball he would have had a bit of fun, then gone off with her money. Who would have thought she could be strong enough to walk away from him and disappear into oblivion so quickly?

That's how he came to be on Gibraltar. He had made some 'friends' inside and was here doing a job for one of them. They wouldn't have been too pleased if he had been caught by the cops last night, fortunately the car he'd used was stolen and wouldn't be traced back to him.

He didn't think the guy who hit him would recognise him, everything had happened so quickly, it wouldn't matter if he did, there would be someone to give him an alibi. Shame though, after waiting all those years for sweet virginal Fay to come across, last night would have been payback time.

Changing into his uniform he looked at his eye again, it was just a black eye, the scratches on his arms were hidden. No problem, he could tell any story he liked. Straightening his cap, he went out onto the deck feeling confident there would be no comeback from last night.

Chapter 16

Emma frowned, strange there was no answer. Perhaps Fay was asleep or had gone for some fresh air to help clear her migraine. I'll leave it till lunch time and pop round then.

Anthony and Leona had gone over to Spain for a few hours which was fortunate because she had an important meeting today. Her mind kept returning to Fay, something was not right, she just felt it. Nathan had been there last night so perhaps she was worrying unnecessarily. Hopefully her meeting would not take long so after that she would call round to Fay's and check on her.

Walking into the Inspector's office Emma looked around for a spare seat and was surprised to see some familiar faces, among them Jerry the croupier from the casino. Inspector Luchiano was in conversation with one of the customs officers but acknowledged her with a slight nod of the head. She walked across to the croupier and sat down on the seat next to him.

"Well I didn't expect to see you again so soon."

He smiled. "No I don't expect you did but then I didn't know we were in the same line of work. Would you like coffee?"

"No thanks, not long since breakfast. So do you know what this is about Jerry?"

"Not yet, but I now know where you got all your information for your books. It often puzzled me how much fact was in your 'fictional novels'."

"I have to say you are some writer Emma."

They both looked towards the door as it opened and several people entered the room.

"Oh it looks like we are about to have our questions answered." Jerry nodded in the direction of the Inspector who was now taking a seat and obviously about to start the briefing.

"Right ladies and gentleman if I can have your attention." Pausing, Inspector Luchiano waited for everyone to stop talking. When when the room was quiet and he had everyone's attention he began the briefing.

"I think you know that this is not a normal briefing, usually we keep you all apart to protect your identities. Due to new information, we've had to bring the operation forward, this briefing was the only way to pass on the information in time for everyone to get organised." He paused.

"We have been informed that we may have a leak in one of our organisations therefore we made the decision to get you all together."

There was a general hum in the room as everyone took in the inspectors words.

Inspector Luchiano waited, allowing his words to sink in, then began his briefing. It took about an hour to ensure every detail had been discussed and everyone was sure what their roles were in this operation. As people left, the Inspector caught Emma's eye and indicated he wanted her to stay. When everyone had gone he asked his secretary to bring in some coffee.

"Sorry to delay you Emma. Have you arranged that meeting yet?"

"Yes, I've got it all in hand. Does he know I am his contact?"

"No, that's why he's not at the meeting. I wanted to let the team know we have reason to believe that someone from inside is passing information on. We have an idea who it is but until we are sure we don't want to act. That's why we have asked for someone outside to be bought in." The inspector paused, giving Emma time to absorb his words.

"Only six people know the identity of your contact; me, you, the customs officers and one undercover officer. To ensure a successful operation we need to ensure there are no more leaks."

He turned to look out the window.

"We picked the five of you carefully because we are confident that none of you are the source of the leak. There is one other agent who is known only by me."

"This has become a major operation, having someone out there unrecognised is our biggest asset. They are in a lot of danger Emma, so keep me informed will you?"

"Of course, and thanks for the coffee." Emma's mind was already working as she walked from the Inspector's office.

Well that was amazing, Jerry being an undercover cop; he didn't seem the type somehow but it confirmed Emma's suspicions that he had been watching Nathan the other night.

Checking out new arrivals – good place to do it the casino.

That was a cryptic comment Luchiano had made regarding her contact. Oh well she would soon know their identity. Right now, time to visit Fay.

Emma had rung the bell several times. Strange there was no answer yet. Fay's car was there. She looked up at the bedroom window but there was no sign of Fay.

'I am really beginning to worry now'.

She walked back to her car, reaching for her mobile she dialled Fay's number. It rang out, so she redialled. After the seventh ring, Fay answered.

"Fay, it's Emma. Sorry if I am disturbing you, I was concerned and wanted to make sure you're OK?"

"Actually Emma I don't feel great, this migraine has been pretty bad. I'm just staying in bed for the day, hopefully I'll feel better tomorrow."

Although she knew she couldn't face Emma, Fay couldn't help thinking that this was the second time she had lied to her. What is happening to me? I hate telling anyone lies, especially to someone I consider my greatest friend.

"Can I do anything, get a doctor to call or something?" Emma asked sensing Fay was being evasive. "Perhaps I should come in and see if I can help."

"Honestly Emma, there is no need. I just need to rest until things improve. Sorry about last night. We can rearrange things for another evening soon." Silently she was pleading with Emma to go away. "Really, I will be fine, I'll call you as soon as I feel more human, thanks for checking on me, bye." She put the phone down before Emma could say anything else.

Whilst Emma was not fooled by Fay, she had other things that needed her attention right now. I will have a word with Nathan later, see if knows what is going on. Very out of character this, but she slipped the car into gear and set off towards the harbour.

Chapter 17

Nathan took every precaution to make sure he was not seen entering the customs house as he walked up to the office and knocked on the door. A chair scraped as someone stood up, then he heard footsteps crossing the wooden floor. When the door opened he was relieved to see the person in front of him matched the photo he had been given.

"Good Morning, Chris Trun I believe."

The man standing in the doorway looked at him questioningly.

Nathan held out his hand. "Nathan Mackenzie. I believe you were told to expect me."

Chris Trun gestured for him to enter the room and closed the door behind him.

"Yes, now I recognize you from the description I was given. Though I am surprised you came to the office."

He gestured towards a chair and turned to adjust the blinds.

"Just a precaution, the window faces onto the jetty. We don't want anyone seeing you and getting nosy. Strangers tend to attract attention among the islanders."

Nathan nodded and sat down.

"I needed some information quickly so I decided to come in person, didn't want to waste time. I decided to take the risk of contacting you here."

Nathan had a feeling something was not right. He wasn't sure but Chris Trun seemed put out by his visit. Unexpected or not, he should have been prepared for some contact to be made.

"Anyway, it is highly unlikely anyone will know me on the island even if they did take an interest in my presence." Nathan sat back in the chair.

"I want information on a couple of yachts in the marina and the crew. I've written down the name and registration of one yacht I am particularly interested in. I would have taken a photo but I didn't want to be noticed." He passed the slip of paper over the desk watching Chris's reactions.

"Did you go to the briefing this morning?"

Chris picked up the paper, gave it a cursory glance and placed it in a folder.

"OK, no problem, I will get onto it right away. Yes, I was at the briefing so I am up to speed, is there anything else you need?"

"No that's all, just let me have that information as soon as you can." There seemed little else to say so he stood and stretched his arm across the desk to shake Chris's hand. "Nice to meet you Chris, no doubt we will be seeing each other again soon. By the way let's keep this information between the two of us for the moment, OK?"

Chris nodded. "OK, any particular reason?"

"Well it is possible it's a wild goose chase and I wouldn't like to ruffle a rich yacht owner's feathers unnecessarily. You know what the bosses are like especially if one of the owners is a friend."

Nathan sensed that Chris was relieved he was leaving. Odd, very odd. Chris had seemed surprised to see him as well, although he should have been expecting him to get in contact soon, but perhaps not in person. He didn't seem surprised by his request for information on the yacht or the crew. Never questioned why Nathan was interested in either.

In fact, Chris Trun had seemed a little nervous, even hostile. But for what reason? Well, Chris would have to wait till later. Right now he had other things to think about. He had to sort a few things before his meeting in the morning. There were one or two things still bothering him and he wanted to get them straight in his mind before meeting his contact. For the moment Chris Trun was forgotten.

Nathan again wondered who his contact would be. The croupier perhaps, who seemed to take an interest in me at the casino. He would know the hotel well so could have left the notes easily without being noticed. Oh well, no point in going over it, all would become clear soon when he met his contact. He walked leisurely, heading back to the hotel, enjoying the warmth of the sun and the wonderful views. When he got to the hotel he realised that he had some free time.

He wanted to check on Fay tomorrow, give her a day to get things sorted in her mind. Which was best, to call round or phone? Perhaps some flowers. Yes, call round with some flowers tomorrow.

After breakfast Nathan decided he would take one of the boat trips round the island before visiting Fay. Maybe that would help familiarize him with some of the places where small boats could come ashore. Unfortunately, when he went to the harbour to book a trip, he couldn't get on a boat till later in the day, so decided to call on Fay first.

Fay ignored the bell but whoever it was not going away. Then it rang again.

'I can't hide for ever,' she told herself. Crossing to the window she peeped out to check who was there. When she saw it was Nathan her face flushed with embarrassment, and again she thought about not answering the door. Then realising she would have to face him sometime, decided it might as well be now. As she walked to the door, she had no idea what she was going to say to him.

When he handed her flowers she felt tears begin to well up. Quickly turning away from him, trying to regain control of her emotions.

"I thought you might need a bit of company, Fay, but if I'm intruding I'll go. Mind, I have brought something to eat as I didn't think you would bother yourself."

He held up a bag which was obviously filled with food, and waited for her to speak.

She was about to say she wanted to be left alone but something in his expression stopped her.

"Thank you, please come in, I was going to call you later to thank you and explain..."

Nathan held up his hand, stopping her in mid-sentence. "No need Fay, no one has the right to assault someone. I'm just glad I came along when I did. Come on I'm starving, let's eat." He gently touched her arm and felt her flinch before she turned to walk in front of him into the lounge. Damn, I should have known not to touch her, he thought as he followed her.

Slowly as they ate their lunch and sipped the wine, Fay relaxed. Nathan was so easy to talk to and she soon felt at ease with him. He only referred to the previous night once to ask if she was OK.

That's when she told him that Thomas was an ex-boyfriend from England and that she had left England hoping never to see him again, certainly never thinking he would visit Gibraltar. Fay couldn't explain how he found her or why he would want to, but that once she opened the door she couldn't keep him out.

Although Fay didn't seem to notice, tears were rolling down her cheeks. Nathan handed her his handkerchief.

"Leave it, Fay, it is over. He's probably off the island by now."

He wanted to reach out and comfort her, to hold her, make her feel safe but knew from similar situations that he had encountered in his work, that this was the last thing Fay would want. She needed time to come to terms with the feelings of vulnerability and all the other emotions which she was surely feeling.

"Come on, let's finish lunch and work out what you are going to tell Emma." The misery in her eyes was painful to see. "Just remember this is not your fault. He attacked you, there was no way you could have stopped him. Fay, you could never have fought him off."

Chapter 18

Fay was still not sure how Nathan had managed to persuade her to go on the boat trip with him. He'd started with, 'It's no good hiding in the house, you will only brood on things and get things out of proportion'. Then he'd said, 'I will be there Fay, you will be safe with me. The sooner you deal with your fears the better, trust me.'

Somehow he managed to convince her that she needed some fresh air to help blow away some of the cobwebs. A change of scene would help her to rationalize what had happened and perhaps help her to deal with her emotions.

Then as they talked, she thought he was right. I have to face Emma tomorrow or do some explaining. Sitting alone, worrying, jumping at every little noise, didn't seem the better option and it might give her mind something else to focus on for a while. So here she was on her way to take a boat trip round the island.

Nathan had helped her find a strength that she had not known existed, helped her to realise things could have been far worse. Regaining control of her life was the way forward. Thomas would not get near her again, not now she knew he was around. He may be miles away by now and if not she would be more careful if their paths crossed. For the moment she felt safe with Nathan and anyway hiding away wasn't going to solve anything anymore than running away had.

Fay roused from her thoughts and realised they were approaching the quay. She tensed. 'What if someone saw her bruises or if Emma saw her. Worst still, what if Thomas hadn't left and they bumped into him.' Her mind began to imagine all sorts of scenario's.

Sensing her nervousness Nathan said "Do you want to go home? I know this can't be easy." He slowed down waiting for her reply.

In her head she was shouting 'Yes! Yes!'

"No, you are right I have to face up to this and the sooner the better." Her face had paled and her expression didn't match her brave words.

Nathan smiled. "Don't worry Fay, I will take care of you. When you want to go home just say and we will do so without hesitation. OK?"

Fay nodded and smiled, trying hard not to show the nervousness inside her whilst chiding herself for being such a wimp.

Nathan parked a little way from the mooring used by sightseeing boats. As they walked along the jetty be noticed that the yacht he'd been interested in had sailed. He didn't want to believe Fay was involved but had hoped to watch her for any reaction when she saw the yacht.

'Why hadn't Chris let me know it had put to sea?' He'd asked to be kept informed regarding the yachts. He'd need to speak to Chris later to find out where the yacht was heading and when it had sailed. He turned his attention back to Fay.

As they reached the pleasure boat Nathan saw Anthony and Leona just boarding. He turned to attract Fay's attention to warn her, but she was lost in her own thoughts and looking out over the sparkling azure sea. Then it was too late, as Anthony turned to help Leona on board, and saw them.

"Well what a coincidence seeing you two. Are you taking the boat trip?"

Leona looked round to see who he was talking to.

"Oh, how lovely, come on sit beside us we can have a good chat." she patted the seats next to her. "Such a shame about the meal the other night, are you feeling better now?"

There was no option but to head for the seat next to Leona. Stepping aboard, Fay felt a sinking feeling deep in the pit of her stomach. She smiled at Leona as she sat down.

"Nathan thought that a sea trip might clear my head, but yes I am much better, sorry to have spoilt the evening."

She had worn a long-sleeved mint green top which covered up the bruises on her arms, but was still painfully aware that, close up, Leona might notice discolouration around her mouth and also sense her nervousness.

In an attempt to avoid this, Fay quickly engaged Leona in conversation about the wedding, hoping to distract her.

Leona had noticed that Fay was trying to hide her face. She waited till the boat rocked slightly causing Fay to change position and took a quick glance at her. It was long enough to see the bruising.

'Hmm, it certainly didn't look like a migraine was the reason for cancelling the dinner, and how come Nathan is suddenly so friendly with Fay?' Leona decided to say nothing but her mind was working overtime.

Anthony watched the two girls chatting like old friends.

"Good looking girl, isn't she?"

On seeing the look that crossed Nathan's face, he said, "OK, keep my nose out, got the message." Changing the subject, he turned his attention to the coastline.

The remainder of the trip was uneventful. Anthony and Nathan took an interest in the coastline, commenting on the ruggedness and the tiny little inlets, whilst the girls chatted about weddings, honeymoons etc. Leona noticed her companion's nervousness. Obviously the bruising had something to do with it. She couldn't help wondering how Fay had got them.

She had taken a liking to Fay. Anthony would tell her not to be so quick to like people but she felt drawn to her. She really hoped her judgement wasn't wrong.

Nathan glanced at the girls, pleased when he saw how well Fay handled the situation. She was probably horrified at meeting Leona and Anthony. Apart from sitting in a position to shield her face with the shadow of her sun hat, she was acting fairly normally. The attack could have been worse, but nevertheless she had been assaulted and badly frightened. Fay was obviously a lot tougher than she looked.

Deep inside, Nathan knew that he was attracted to her and that she was reaching a part of him he had tried to close forever. How many times since meeting her had he told himself to be careful, keep your distance, especially now after all she was currently a suspect. Keeping his distance was proving harder than he thought. Easy to say be careful, don't get involved… doing it was a different thing altogether.

After the trip, Leona suggested they all had coffee together, but Fay said she was feeling a little tired and asked Nathan to drive her home. As they drove away, looking back to wave, Leona and Anthony were already eagerly comparing notes on Fay's bruises and Nathan's protective air. It was obvious to them both that something was not quite right with Fay and when had Nathan and Fay become friends.

When they arrived at her house she thanked him for the trip but when she opened the car door she hesitated. Nathan saw Fay look at the house, her eyes filled with tears. Reaching out slowly, he took hold of her hand and gently stroked her arm.

"It will feel safe again, don't let that man take away your home."

Getting out of the car Fay smiled at him then looked away, she didn't want him to see the fear in her eyes. She walked to the door, unlocked it then turned and waved before shutting it behind her.

Nathan waited a few minutes until he saw Fay walk past the lounge window. Should he stay just to make sure she was OK? But before he could make up his mind, Fay looked out and waved at him. He waved back and drove back towards the hotel. Try as he might he could not see her being involved in drugs. She seemed a little naïve, and at times he sensed she was keeping a part of her life hidden. Still he just didn't see her as a smuggler.

His judgement could be influenced by the sympathy he felt for her… Oh blast! I have to concentrate on the job and not Fay.

He turned and began to study the map, chiding himself for letting his guard down.

Chapter 19

The map reference he'd been given was easy to locate. It looked like it was one of the Moorish towers that were on the island. His mind kept straying back to Fay. Her friend had not seemed the type to be scared off easily. The yacht had gone and so hopefully he had as well. Then again, if the yacht was involved he would most certainly return. He hoped her ex-boyfriend didn't decide to pay her another visit, when he might not be there to help. Right now, he had a meeting to go to.

Nathan waited for his contact and tried to look like a tourist. He'd been to see the apes again before going to the meeting point. He had been there several minutes when he saw someone walking towards him. As they drew closer he was sure he recognised who it was but couldn't believe she could be involved.

"Hello Nathan, sorry to spring this on you. I am aware of the need to protect your identity." Emma smiled. "I'm sure you didn't expect to see me."

Nathan was obviously surprised at her appearance. "Emma? You are my contact? Well I shouldn't be surprised. Really you are an obvious candidate. Does Anthony know your line of business?"

They both stepped into the shade of the tower even this early in the day it was hot.

"No, only you, and I would prefer it if you didn't tell him. Come on, we don't have much time so let's get down to business. This is the information I have been able to obtain from our informant." They both knelt down and got on with exchanging details and making plans to catch the smugglers in the act. When they had covered everything, Nathan stood up to leave. Emma touched his arm to delay him.

"By the way, have you seen Fay today? I spoke to her earlier but she didn't seem to want to see me. Any idea what is going on?"

He smiled. "Oh she's OK, still feeling a little fragile but I called earlier and took her out for some fresh air. In fact, we bumped into Anthony and Leona. You and Fay seem very close, Emma. What's her story?"

"I have never asked her. When she came for her interview I sensed she was lonely, unhappy. Her CV was good and I liked her, so I took her on. She's never given me cause to regret my decision and yes, I am very fond of her. I feel that she is part of my family. Why do you ask?"

"Just general interest. After all, Emma, she is an attractive girl." Nathan hoped Emma would accept his answer, he didn't want to reveal his doubts about Fay just yet. Emma wasn't the type of woman to be easily fooled and would surely have known if Fay was involved in anything shady.

"Well I'll be off, be in touch with you soon."

He looked around from the entrance to make sure no one was about before he waved to Emma. As he stepped into the open he felt the warmth of the sun on his body causing him to shiver. Then, casting a quick glance around to double check he was not being watched, he left the tower.

Emma watched him walk away, she also shivered; the towers were always cool but that was not the cause of her shiver. It was obvious something was not right. Nathan seemed to be checking on Fay. Emma searched her mind trying to find anything that could explain why Nathan was suspicious of Fay, but nothing came to mind. Maybe I'm wrong, he may be interested in getting to know her better. She looked around the tower making sure they had left nothing and then walked out into the sunshine. At the moment she had more urgent things than Fay's romantic involvements to occupy her mind.

Fay felt better for the fresh air, though her head was pounding and some of her muscles were still aching from her struggle with Thomas. She walked into the kitchen to look for some pain killers. Just as she reached up to the cupboard she thought she heard a noise. Turning round quickly she glanced around the room, her heart pounding. No, there was nobody there and she had locked the door behind her. Still she felt edgy and could feel her pulse racing.

Silently she chided herself. 'I'm just being silly, feeling spooked.' She turned and picked up a glass then as she filled it with water the doorbell rang. The glass slid through her fingers, dropped to the floor and shattered on the tiles. A pool of water quickly spread across the floor. She stood still, not wanting to answer the door. She could hear the her heart pounding in her head as it began to race. Then just as she was about to totally lose it she heard Leona call out.

"Are you OK Fay?"

Stepping over the glass and spilt water she went to open the door.

"Sorry Leona, I've just dropped a glass. Yes, I am fine. Come in."

"I thought I heard a noise. Not cut yourself I hope."

Why was she so jumpy? Leona could see the bruise more clearly now even though Fay had attempted to cover the bruising on her face with make-up.

Fay shook her head, knowing how on edge she was, hoping Leona would not stay too long or ask any awkward questions.

"Excuse me, I need to dry the floor; being tiled it is easy to slip. It's lovely to see you and a nice surprise." Fay hoped she sounded convincing.

"I hope you don't mind me just dropping in. I was in need of some company. Anthony has gone off somewhere and Emma is out. I was hoping you wouldn't mind me coming round uninvited, but if you have seen enough of me today or are busy I will get out of your hair." She looked hopefully at Fay.

Fay smiled. "Don't be silly, just let me clear this glass away and then I will make us a drink." As she walked into the kitchen she found herself feeling relieved that she would not be on her own for a while. Her nerves were obviously still very much on edge having Leona here would give her something else to think about. She made the drinks and took them into the lounge.

"Would you like something to eat, Leona?"

Leona declined and it was not long before they were both engrossed in conversation. Mainly about the wedding but also the boat trip. Leona seemed captivated by the island, especially the wonderful coastline with all the coves and the high craggy rocks. She thought it was beautiful and did capture the imagination. Seeing it for the first time was always a thrill.

Fay felt that something seemed to have changed in Leona's attitude toward her. She couldn't quite put her finger on it but she seemed uncomfortable and a bit guarded.

'Oh, it's just me, I'm putting my tension onto her'. Fay mentally shook herself and tried to relax whilst Leona chattered on.

Chapter 20

Anthony got back to the house to find his mother sipping tea and reading the newspaper.

"Where is Leona?"

"She was out when I got back but she left a note to say she was going to see Fay for a chat. Nice they get along isn't it."

"Yes, but bit late to go visiting though. Still, it gives us time together Mum. I'll get some more tea and then we can have a good talk."

Nathan got back to the hotel to find another note under his door. He hated working blind, he liked to assess the people he worked with, build up some kind of trust. So far the information he received had been genuine and reliable but the informant was still unknown, so they were not what Nathan called 'a reliable source'. He hoped Inspector Luchiano's faith in the source was justified. Throwing his jacket on the bed he poured a drink and sat down to read the note.

Smiling to himself, he wondered what Anthony would say if he knew about his mother's secret. At least he knew Emma was a reliable contact.

Damn!

He would have to speed things up, it looked as if the smugglers had been spooked and were planning to bring the operation forward. If the informant was to be believed things were already on the move and could be taking off tonight. Walking over to the table he sat down thinking of who to contact. Not everyone was in the loop and he didn't want to arouse suspicion unnecessarily. Picking up the phone he dialled Emma's number.

It was getting late; Anthony and Emma had begun to wonder when Leona would be back. "I think I'll ring Fay, Mum. I expected Leona to be back by now."

Anthony let the phone ring several times but there was no reply. The expression on his face told Emma how concerned he was.

"Perhaps they have gone for a drink and lost track of time. We can try again shortly and if there is no reply then go round to check on them." Emma smiled at the look of concern on her son's face.

"I'm sure they are fine." 'What it is to be in love.' she thought.

They both jumped as the phone rang. Emma answered it.

"Oh hello, yes of course that is fine. I'll meet you there, and I'll let the others know the meeting time has been changed. Bye."

"One of my ladies' meetings. I need to ring round, Anthony. Sorry."

"Don't worry mum. I think I'll take a drive to Fay's and pick up Leona. I need to do some work when I get back anyway." He picked up the car keys and waved as he walked out of the door. "See you later."

As he drove up hill towards Fay's house Anthony was going over possible reasons why he had no reply from Fay. Leona would usually text him if she thought she would be later than expected.

As if someone had read his thoughts! His phone bleeped. 'OK, I'm worrying about nothing. This will be Leona saying she is at home'. He looked for somewhere to stop and read the text.

He was passing the graveyard where some of the sailors from the battle of Trafalgar were buried. It was an awkward spot. There was nowhere to stop immediately, and as soon as he could, he pulled over. Picking up his mobile he opened the text, it wasn't from Leona or Fay.

It was from his boss advising him to go to a meeting to get some information about the job. Anthony read the text again. It was clear something unexpected had happened. 'Blast I won't have time to check on the girls.'

He couldn't ignore the message despite his concern for Leona. After a few moments thought, he sent a text message to both Fay and Leona asking one of them to get back to him as soon as possible. He might have to make up a story if Fay got in touch but he needed to know where Leona was. She would be in hot water if he didn't find her soon. Putting his concern to the back of his mind he slipped the car into gear and set off to meeting.

As it turned out the meeting proved to be more important than he had thought, although an unknown contact had left a message and not come in person. The operation had been bought forward, the drop was expected tonight and the informant had evidence that led him to believe that arms would be involved.

Once everything had been arranged and every detail gone over Anthony checked his phone. Still no message, he was beginning to think something was wrong, Leona knew better than to be out of contact with him.

He sent a text message to his office advising them that Leona was out of contact and he would be proceeding on his own. He just hoped that the girls were OK. Perhaps they had got talking and forgotten the time or had a few glasses of wine and Leona had decided to stay at Fay's. Leona was normally very good at keeping him informed of her whereabouts, to the point that it sometimes drove him crazy. He tried to put his concerns to the back of his mind and headed off to pick up some things he needed.

Nathan picked up the map. Fortunately he had managed to contact Emma and had got the office to send a text for an operative to collect details of the smugglers' movements. No one had expected things to move so quickly, still he was as ready as he was ever going to be. He couldn't help wondering what had spooked the smugglers. Could it be the leak that everyone, quite rightly, was so concerned about? There had been some discussion about someone on the inside passing on information but to his knowledge, so far nothing had been found to confirm this.

The idea that a colleague would give information to criminals disturbed everyone. It affected morale, caused tension and mistrust between colleagues. Just what the crooks wanted.

He patted his shoulder checking his gun was there, looked at the time and then left to meet his colleague.

Chapter 21

Anthony looked around, checking for any other vehicles hidden in the shadows before cautiously driving into the moonlit bay. He was expecting another officer to join him but there was no sign of anyone, just a small boat moored nearby, the moonlight catching its shadow as it gently drifted on the water.

He turned his lights off, the moon was bright enough for him to see. He manoeuvred the car into the shadows to ensure he was hidden from view, leaving the key in the ignition, just in case he needed to make a hasty exit. Sitting in the shadows every sound was menacing, even a fly which had somehow got into the car and kept buzzing him. Although he was used to this kind of surveillance, once or twice he found himself suddenly alert and peering into the darkness, then realising it was only imagination or a bird on the cliffs squawking. He checked again that he had locked the doors and patted the gun which lay in his lap, then turned back to stare into the darkness of the bay.

After about 15 minutes he began to think his instructions were wrong, something should be happening by now. Perhaps the informant's information was wrong. Seconds later he was alert. Holding his breath, he listened intently, there was movement to the left of the car. His hand went to his gun but before he could pick it up a voice startled him.

"Surprised to see you here, Anthony, care to explain?"

Looking towards the car door he could just see the top of someone's head as they crouched down by the car.

"Are you going to let me in? I don't relish being out here all night."

Anthony unlocked the door and Nathan slipped into the passenger seat.

"We are on the same side, I hope. You're not here for some secret assignation that I won't be able to tell Leona about, are you?" Nathan laughed quietly. He had been informed that Anthony was a member of the Customs, and wrong footed his friend.

"I hope we are on the same side otherwise this could get awkward, and no you won't have to explain anything to Leona." Anthony smiled.

"Sorry Nathan. I didn't know your line of work either. You know how important secrecy is for all of us."

In the darkness, Anthony felt a slight movement in the air as Nathan nodded in agreement to his statement. "We think there may be a leak somewhere in the department. Until we had some idea who the source is no one talked to anyone about this operation. You know as well as me that if your cover had been blown you would have been in danger."

Nathan whispered, "Looks like we're on," as he picked up his gun. Nathan knew Anthony was right, they both worked undercover in dangerous situations any leak was hazardous to them and other team members.

"So was all this about a wedding a farce?"

"I'm working for Customs, assigned to the drug squad at the moment, and just in case you think I haven't been straight with you, our friendship means a lot to me." Anthony paused. Nathan would know by the end of the operation that Leona was a member of the drugs team, so he couldn't see any harm in telling him about her part in the operation.

"Leona and I sometimes work as a team; the wedding is our cover story."

"Really, how come…" Nathan didn't get chance to finish his sentence. At that moment, there was movement in the darkness near the moored boat. They both became very still. It wasn't long till they were certain someone was creeping about in the shadows, moving slowly alongside the boat. The bright moonlight was acting as a torch for them.

They both sat watching, straining to hear any sounds, their guns ready in case of trouble. As the cloud cleared, a moonlit figure moved closer to the mooring and started to untie the boat, occasionally glancing over their shoulder. Fortunately, their car was hidden in the shadow of a large outcrop of rock, so they were not spotted.

"Looks like our information was right. As soon as he gets out of sight we go over the top, in the lee of the ridge, to the caves, we should be in time to give the signal." Anthony whispered, shifting his position, preparing to leave the car.

Nathan said nothing, but nodded as he watched the figure manoeuvre the boat into the water.

They heard the muffled sound of oars being put into the rowlocks and then the sound of splashing water as the oars were pulled through the sea. As the boat sailed out of sight, they stepped quietly out of the car, crouching beside it until they could risk making for the rocks. The moon seemed to be on their side, and as it went behind a cloud they moved forward, keeping in the shadows as they made their way across the rocks. It wasn't easy to keep low to the ground and move quickly but they needed to stay in the shadows in case anyone was watching. It didn't take too long before they were headed up and along the path over the cliff top towards the caves.

Unseen eyes were already watching the caves.

Emma and the Inspector were keeping watch together, Jerry and Chris were nearer the cave entrance hiding in the shadows and keeping out of sight. They had seen some men enter the caves and were just waiting for the signal to let them know the boat had sailed and that Nathan and Anthony were on their way.

"If our information is right the boat should be leaving the cove by now. The others will be on their way, and they will only get one chance to signal. Watch for it, Emma, we don't want to miss it." Luchiano whispered.

They continued to peer into the darkness over the rocks for any sign of movement. It seemed to be a long time and Emma was beginning to think something was wrong, then she saw movement, looking harder she saw the signal.

"Look there, it's the signal." Emma pointed towards the cliff. "That means the boat has sailed and Nathan is on his way."

It was a relief to them both as it meant their informant's information was correct and the smugglers were definitely making their move tonight.

Chapter 22

Fay and Leona were cold and very frightened; they couldn't understand what had happened. One minute they were having a chat and a drink, then the door had been battered in, and two armed and hooded men were standing in front of them. The men said nothing, grabbing the girls and waving the gun in their faces, and making a shushing sound to indicate they should be quiet. They needn't have bothered, the shock and the sight of guns made sure of their silence.

The men put hoods over the girls' heads and tied them up. The fact the men did not speak was menacing and the hoods increased their fear, being unable to see their attackers. Then they were suddenly lifted up.

Leona felt the fresh air as they were carried out of the house, before being thrown down onto a floor which seemed to shake under them. They heard an engine start and felt movement; obviously they were in some kind of vehicle.

Fay tried to whisper to Leona as the vehicle moved but was slapped across the face. Someone made a shushing noise close to her ear. Feeling dizzy and frightened, she deciding not to attempt to speak again.

It seemed they were driving for ages, then the vehicle stopped and they heard the doors open. They were dragged out, pushed forwards, falling onto some rough ground. As Fay tried to pick herself up she felt sharp pieces of rock under her knees and hands. She heard Leona's sharp intake of breath and assumed she had also fallen on the uneven ground. Once standing they were pushed and dragged along, as the ground evened out they were urged to move faster.

The temperature had dropped and it was really cold. Fay tripped and put her tied hands out in an effort to steady herself. She felt what appeared to be a wall of rock. It was damp and a little slimy. Could they be in some kind of cave? There were a lot of caves in Gibraltar. Fear was beginning to take control of her and she started to shake. Unable to stop, she could only imagine Leona was feeling the same. They were in a cave. It smelt damp and musty and seemed to echo their stumbling steps. That would explain the rough path and the cold, damp feel to the air.

Leona was just as frightened and was concerned that Fay may be hurt. She hadn't heard her make a sound since her attempt to speak earlier. Like Fay, she was unable to do anything but follow the silent instructions the men were giving them. She could hear Fay's breathing and was just glad they were still together. Her training was telling her to obey the men and not risk getting hurt by annoying them, but her fear was urging her against caution. She wanted to defend herself and protect Fay, although at the moment she had no way of fighting back.

Suddenly she felt the surface level out and there was fresh air blowing around them. Somehow though, Leona didn't feel the ground was steady beneath her. Then her tied hands were grabbed and she was violently thrown to the floor. She felt the ground beneath her shudder, it didn't make sense, she couldn't work out where they were.

Leona listened, hoping to hear Fay's voice. Within seconds she felt the floor vibrate and heard sounds of struggling. Was that Fay? Perhaps they were tying her up near her? She heard a gasp and then Fay speaking to someone, her voice shaky and tearful.

"You! Why? What do you want from me?"

Someone laughed but didn't reply to Fay's question.

"Please let her go. She has done nothing to you." There was a tremor in Fay's voice as she uttered the last few words.

Leona realised that Fay had seen her tied up nearby, and that she seemed to know whoever had abducted them. Her mind began to whirl, she had so many questions all of which would remain unanswered for the time being.

Then Leona heard a harsh laugh and a man's voice. "I didn't get what I wanted from you, did I? Still a frigid little virgin are you, or has someone finally made you into a woman? Maybe that bloke I ran into." The sneering voice hesitated.

"Anyway, things have changed, the people I am working for heard about our little 'affair' and thought you would be useful to them."

There was a dull thud and the ground seemed to move again, then Leona heard Fay gasp.

"You two are our insurance and if you want to get through this you will do as you are told. My friends don't mess about. One false move and you both die."

Fay watched as Thomas walked over to Leona. Fearing he was going to hurt her, she sobbed as she shouted, "No, please no." Knowing she couldn't do anything to stop him.

He looked back at her and smiled then he reached down and removed the hood from Leona's head. Leona jumped as the hood was pulled off. It was dark and at first she couldn't focus. Then slowly, as her eyes adjusted to the dim light, figures came into view and she could just see Fay's outline.

"Fay, are you OK?" Her head spun as one of the men slapped her.

"Keep your mouth shut and don't try to escape. She's tied to the rails, almost hanging over the edge, one slip and she will be gone."

The man pointed to Fay then laughed. "Don't cause us any trouble, do you hear?" He turned, walking into the darkness then shouted. "If you do you'll be close behind her, and that's a promise."

This was not looking good. The fact that they were quite happy to hit her and Fay was an indication the men were violent and would use force, seemingly without much provocation.

Leona couldn't see a way out of this situation, and what concerned her more was that Fay seemed to know one of the men. Leona felt sure Fay was not the criminal type but she also knew everyone had a breaking point. Maybe Fay had problems that would explain the bruising and her nervousness. Had she had been duped into helping these men. Were the doubts about Fay founded after all? No, she couldn't believe that Fay was involved, even though she definitely knew one of the smugglers. There has to be some explanation. If she heard right, he mentioned an affair. But Fay wasn't the type to have affairs.

As Leona mulled things over, she became more unsure about Fay and more certain that escaping was not going to be easy, especially as she wasn't sure she could rely on Fay to help her. The men had left a small oil lantern which gave a small glimmer of light in the cave but it was not enough to help Leona to see anything that gave her any hope of escape.

Now they were alone, Fay looked across to Leona, hoping to speak to her. She caught Leona looking in her direction, started to speak then stopped. In the dimness of the cave she thought she saw Leona shake her head indicating that they should do as they were told and keep quiet.

The lack of light had begun to unnerve Fay, she was frightened, her mouth was dry and she felt near to tears. After her last encounter with Thomas she was terrified of what he might have planned for her. She pulled against the ropes but to no avail, any movement seemed to make the ground underneath them shake. She guessed they were on a viewing platform which stuck out from the wall of one of the caves she had visited many times. It was cold and the wind was whistling around them. If she was right, there was a very long drop beneath them. Perhaps Leona was right, it wasn't a good idea to antagonise these men.

For some time neither of the girls spoke or moved. The cold breeze wafted around them and it wasn't long before they both started to shiver. The constant breeze and the dampness was getting into their bones, adding to the fear building inside them.

Fay could hear the men talking and realised they were still near but their voices had got a lot quieter, presumably they had moved some distance away. She decided to try whispering to Leona again: try to explain how she knew Thomas, how sorry she was that Leona had got involved, this could be her last chance. Hoping Leona would hear her before they did she decided to risk whispering.

"I'm sorry Leona, it's my fault you are here. Keep positive. I'm sure Anthony will be looking for you by now. I want to…" She heard the quiet shush noise Leona made indicating that they should remain silent. She stopped whispering, not wanting to bring Thomas and his friend back, but her mind was working overtime. Why was he doing this, what good were they to him and his friends? He had said they were insurance, against what? Something obviously illegal, but what exactly?

Fay knew that Thomas could be violent and didn't want to give him cause to hurt her or Leona. Still, she was struggling to understand why he was doing this. He was the one who had been the cause of their break up. Surely he was not blaming her, trying to get his own back? If they had married, he would have committed bigamy and eventually Fay would have found out. Who were these friends he mentioned and how was Thomas involved with them?

Panic began to take hold, her fear increased the more she tried to reason things out. She couldn't even begin to see a way out. The same question kept revolving round in her head. How was this going to end?

Thomas was angry and had already shown that he was aggressive. He seemed to think she had been responsible for whatever had happened to him since they parted. Well in a way she probably was. Perhaps someone more worldly-wise would have given him time to divorce Debra and then married him. Unfortunately for him, she was very young and had no experience of men and thought her relationship with Thomas was the greatest romance of all time.

'What a stupid idiotic fool I was.' Tears began to well in her eyes and as hard as she tried to stop them, they slowly trickled down her cheeks. 'Now I have involved Leona all because of a silly schoolgirl romance.'

The breeze wafted the smell from the oil lamp in her direction, it irritated her nose and she felt a wave of nausea go through her. She felt total and utter despair, and this time Nathan wasn't around to save her. Get a grip, she told herself, but easier said than done.

There seemed to be no way out of situation, no happy ending and the more she tried to find some hope, the worse each scenario became. It was pretty obvious to Fay that Thomas could be violent, and presumably so could his companions. She had to keep her wits about her otherwise there was no telling what was in store for them both.

Trying to keep calm and fight the fear that was coursing through her, Fay imagined ways they might escape. She had to keep her fear under control and be ready to take any opportunity which made escape possible. Deep down she didn't believe escape was feasible. If only she could talk to Leona together they may be able to work something out.

Leona's mind was also working overtime. She knew that Anthony would be concerned, as they had agreed to make regular contact, and by now he would be wondering where she was. 'Would he think to go to Fay's?' If he did then he would see the signs of forced entry and would suspect something untoward had happened, but would he think they had been abducted? If nothing else, he would flag up the fact that she was not following procedure and may be missing. They had known each other for some time, he knew her to be capable and would expect her to be able to handle most situations, but at the moment she couldn't see how she could do anything other than comply with the kidnappers' orders.

Fay's soft sobbing interrupted her thoughts; she wanted to whisper some words of encouragement but that could antagonise the men even further and possibly lead to more violence.

Leona turned her mind back to their situation trying to recall all the details she had noted since their capture and work out where they were.

Probably underground, because when the men had been talking their voices seem to echo. That, and with the cold air and dampness, she thought they may be in a cave. Although the lack of light could be deliberate, just to unnerve them more. The ground had been rough underfoot and they had been led through a narrow passage by their captors. Could they be members of the smuggling ring that she and Anthony had been tracking? If so they were in real trouble, these were people without any conscience, killing two women would not bother them at all. Perhaps the operation had begun and they were insurance against interference from the police.

Once again, the sound of Fay's sobbing broke through her thoughts. Fay surely was not a part of the gang, but she did seem to know one of the men. It didn't make sense for them to tie her up and treat her so badly if she was involved.

Hopefully, Fay would get a chance to explain how she knew the man; just at the moment that didn't look likely.

Leona pulled her thoughts back to the possibility of escape. 'I need to keep alert and look for the any opportunity.' She pulled against the ropes that were securing her, sighing as she once again realised they were not going to budge. Stay calm, she told herself, that is the only thing we can do. Help could be on the way at this very moment.

Chapter 23

Satisfied they were alone, the smugglers walked over to the cave entrance. Within seconds two more men appeared. They were carrying large boxes, and a third man, close behind them, was carrying some smaller boxes, totally unaware they were being watched.

Nathan noted they didn't seem to be struggling to carry the boxes so they couldn't be heavy. After a few words to each other one of the men went back, heading down towards the inlet whilst the others climbed back up to the cave.

It was difficult to be sure what was happening, there was no longer any natural light from the moon, only some dim light coming from inside the entrance to the cave. Nathan and Anthony watched the smugglers, waiting for the opportunity to move closer.

Nathan whispered. "We'll let them get inside the caves, with a bit of luck we might be able to cut off their exit. Incidentally Anthony, does Emma know what you do?"

"No and I would like it to stay that way." Anthony could imagine what his mother would say if she knew that despite his degree, he had chosen this line of work. He had lied to her, and she hated lies. Compounded by his false engagement to Leona, he knew she would be furious; and Emma furious was a sight to behold.

Telling his mother that he had gone into a similar line of work as his father would have caused Emma even more distress. She had never really got over losing his father and sister, especially as the murderers had never been caught.

"Well I think it's too late for that but I'll let you two sort it out."

Nathan smiled to himself, sure that Emma would become aware of her son's deceit sooner than Anthony knew.

Anthony wasn't sure what Nathan meant but now was no time to discuss it. "Luchiano and his partner should know the area well so we'll have to trust them to follow our lead. There are two men watching the boat, they'll cut the smugglers off if they manage to evade us."

Nathan nodded.

"Jerry and Chris will be in position by now. There's at least three of them, and there may be more inside." Nathan put his hand on Anthony's shoulder. "Go easy mate don't try any heroics. Let's both try to come out of this unscathed."

They edged forward slowly trying to keep the advantage of surprise. As they got close to the cave entrance, Anthony crawled cautiously ahead. He remembered some of the geography of the caves from his youth. He intended to cross the entrance at the narrowest point, keeping close to the wall, leaving Nathan on the right so that both sides of the entrance were covered.

The dim light from the cave was helping him but he knew that it would probably show his shadow if one of the men was looking in his direction.

As he lay flat on the floor, he felt the adrenalin rush which had become so familiar to him when he knew he was in danger. Keeping flat and in the shadow as much as he could, slowly, cautiously, he crossed the entrance, breathing a silent sigh of relief when he reached the other side without being noticed.

Fortunately, the men were too involved in their conversation to hear any slight noise. They seemed to be certain they were safe and were totally absorbed in chatting to their friends.

Once Nathan signalled he was in position, both sides of the entrance would be covered. Looking across the entrance he saw Nathan's signal. Simultaneously they moved slowly forward so they were right at the edge of the entrance to the cave. Jerry and Chris were covering their backs at the entrance of the tunnel, so they were able to dismiss any attack from the rear and concentrate on the men in the cave. Surprise was their biggest advantage and they didn't want to lose it.

The voices became more distinct as they got further in and then they heard something heavy being moved. The noise penetrated the gloomy tunnel making a weird, surreal sound as it echoed past them.

Stopping quickly, they listened for footsteps but no one appeared. Nathan looked across at Anthony who was indicating he was ready to go. The lack of light was in some ways a help to them, if they couldn't see very well in the dim light then presumably neither could the men inside the cave. The gloom of the tunnel behind them might also give them an advantage hiding their sudden appearance. Confusion on this occasion could be their best friend.

Nathan leaned forward a fraction so he could see further into the cave. A shaft of light was coming from the left-hand side of the tunnel. Checking first that Anthony was covering him, he flattened himself to the floor then moved carefully forward to a position where he could get a better look. The men's backs were visible and some boxes stacked against the cave wall, he waited for his eyes to focus.

Crates and boxes were piled haphazardly on top of each other. There were three, no five people moving about. He needed to get closer so he could get a better look. Edging forward slowly he was able to see more clearly.

Yes, now he could see, there were five men, all concentrating on putting something into the large boxes. He couldn't be certain but it looked as if they were small bags or perhaps holdalls. The men were laughing and talking as they worked, obviously not expecting anyone to interrupt them.

Nathan signalled Anthony to wait whilst he tried to hear some of the men's conversation. He thought he heard them mention two women, saying they were behaving. Could they be girlfriends? Perhaps they were coming to meet them here or keeping watch outside. If that was the case the rest of the team would have to deal with them and the man who had gone back to the boat. He and Anthony had their hands full here.

Just as he was about to signal to Anthony to move in, one of the men turned and headed towards the tunnel. Nathan quickly moved back into the shadows but not before he caught a glimpse of him. He was almost certain he recognized the man. He looked a lot like Thomas, the man who attacked Fay.

What was he doing here? Was she involved after all and was one of the women they were discussing? He felt a jolt of fear as he realised she could be in danger.

Thomas had not been too friendly last time he had been with Fay. What if he had hurt her or was planning to do so? If Fay was one of the girls they had been joking about, who was the other one?

Pressing himself against the tunnel walls he looked across to make sure Anthony wasn't visible, signalling that someone was coming out. He just hoped that Anthony understood, the man coming out would pass close to him. Whilst it wasn't easy to see in the gloom Anthony would have little chance to defend himself.

The man walked out of the cave and turned left, straight past Anthony, missing his feet by a few centimetres. He was whistling to himself as he walked up the tunnel unaware he was being observed from the shadows. Nathan only managed to get a glimpse of him but he was certain it was Thomas.

They waited a couple of minutes in case the man came back to the cave. Then, just as they were about to make a move on the four men, a second man turned and headed towards the cave entrance. Anthony couldn't believe his luck, this man just seemed to step over him brushing his hand with his foot as he went by. He must have thought he'd caught a stone on the floor. Breathing a sigh of relief he looked across at Nathan, who also couldn't believe the man had not seen Anthony. Nathan had been ready to go to his rescue but things could have got very messy. It appeared fate was on their side today.

Nathan indicated that now was their chance to tackle the three men still inside the cave. He knew they couldn't get out easily and it was better to tackle them whilst the other two were out of the way. Surprise was on their side. If they were quick they might not need to use their guns, which would give them a chance of surprising the other two men.

When they crawled across the tunnel, two men were standing on the right close together with their backs to the cave mouth, the other man was standing slightly further over to the left intent on checking the bags.

Nathan went in first, rugby tackling the two men nearest, Anthony was hot on his heels but the third man was already aiming a gun at Nathan's back. Anthony threw himself at the man's feet knocking him off balance, the gun went off, the sound reverberating round the cave walls.

Anthony's tackle didn't give the man time to shout out before he was subdued, but the shot would have been heard throughout the cave. The other two men had been completely unaware of their attackers' presence so, taken by surprise, put up little resistance.

Anthony looked over at Nathan, hoping the bullet had not hit him and was relieved to see he was unhurt. Quickly they tied and gagged the three men then looked round for some cover.

The sound of the shots would surely have alerted the two men who had left the cave earlier. No doubt they would return to find out what was going on. Sure enough, within seconds, they heard feet running down the tunnel towards them. Then suddenly they heard a woman's voice calling out for help.

Nathan froze. That sounded like Fay! So, she was here. He looked across to see if Anthony had heard Fay. Anthony nodded, indicating he had heard her, then he flattened himself against the wall of the cave entrance, hoping the two men would run into the cave without checking, their minds focused on helping their friends.

Sure enough one man ran into the cave and stopped dead, surprised at seeing his friends tied up. By the time he recovered enough to think of looking behind him, Anthony had jumped him and was fighting to restrain him.

Nathan had hidden by some boxes and looked on, ready to help. He was waiting for the other man who he believed to be Thomas, to enter the cave. Staying hidden he continued to wait. It didn't take long for him to realise that Thomas was not planning to join the party. He had obviously heard the scuffle as the fourth man was grappled to the ground and decided not to go into the cave. Nathan checked to see if Anthony was OK, then moved to leave the cave.

Keeping in the shadows Nathan edged to the cave entrance and looked out into the tunnel. He couldn't see anyone but as he listened he could hear someone breathing heavily. Obviously whoever it was, they were fairly close.

Lying flat to the ground he slid forward, then as he fully emerged from the cave, rolled sideways pointing his gun down the tunnel. He couldn't actually see anything in the gloom but as he moved forward again a bullet whizzed past him, hitting the wall just above his head. The tunnel echoed with the sound of the shot and he thought he heard someone scream. He rolled back to the comparative safety of the cave entrance.

Anthony was busy securing the last man who was talking nonstop, but glanced over to check that Nathan was OK.

The smuggler was talking but was so shaken that he was not making sense. All Anthony could make out was.

'I tried to reason with him and he won't let her go.'

Chapter 24

Edging forward into the tunnel again, Nathan waited, hoping to get some idea of where the man he believed to be Thomas was.

"If you want to see her alive stay back, I'll kill them both if you get too close." A voice rang out echoing through the tunnel.

Now the smugglers were secured, Anthony went to help Nathan. He relayed the conversation he'd had with the smuggler. "Who the hell is he talking about, Nathan? Have you any idea?" but even as he spoke his mind was filling with fear and the realisation that it could be Leona and Fay.

Nathan shook his head. "I'm not sure, but I think it could be Fay; if so, possibly Leona as well." Nathan could only guess at Anthony's reaction to his words. Anthony had told him about Leona's role in the operation. He also knew that agents working together formed strong bonds, if one of them was in danger the other would do anything to get them out of trouble.

He shouted into the gloom of the tunnel. "Who are you talking about?" His question met with complete silence.

"Listen whoever it is, what's the point of killing anyone? We will get you eventually and then you will be facing a murder charge. Give yourself up man."

There was still no reply.

Nathan edged forward again, Anthony staying close behind him.

Peering down the tunnel neither of them could see anything. Then they thought they heard movement. Staying perfectly still for a few seconds, they listened, hoping to hear the noise again. As their eyes adjusted to the darkness, Nathan pointed to a dark shadow which seemed to be moving towards them. They waited to make sure it wasn't a trick of the light.

It seemed a long time, but eventually they could see for certain it was a shadow, and it was moving slowly down the tunnel towards them.

Was Thomas trying to lure them closer, get them out in the open so he could kill them? Either way they had to go forward. If he had the girls then they had to keep moving towards him. It was the only way they had any hope of rescuing them. As they drew closer the shadow became still and seemed to get smaller. It looked like a bundle of rubbish on the cave floor, then the sound of a female voice reached them.

"He has a gun and will use it." Leona cried out.

"Please be careful. He's still got Fay. He let me go but I don't think he will release her."

Anthony felt a chill of fear as he recognized Leona's voice. Cautiously they crept closer to her, expecting to be shot at any moment, but there was no challenge from the man they believed to be Thomas. Moving slowly towards her along the tunnel, Leona had heard them and was trying to crawl to meet them. When they were close enough both Nathan and Thomas lifted her, carrying her back down the tunnel to get some distance between them and the gunman.

Nathan talked to Leona to reassure her she was safe, undoing the ropes whilst Anthony held her, trying get her to talk slower so that he could understand what she was saying.

Before they could completely free her she was pulling away and trying to go back up the tunnel.

"Find Fay, he has taken Fay. He's tied her to the platform, he won't let her go." Anthony knew she was desperate to go back and help Fay, but he held her firmly.

"I'm sure he's going to kill her." Leona tried to pull away, intent on going back to help, but Anthony kept his hold.

"You have to help her, Anthony. He's mad, so angry with her, I know he won't let her go."

He had worked with Leona before and knew that she was not one to imagine things. If she thought Fay was in serious danger, then it was more than likely so.

"Leona, you stay here. We will go after him and help Fay."

She shook her head still trying to free herself. "I must go to her, he will kill her. I can't leave her there on her own with him," she said, trying to get out of Anthony's grasp. "It's my job to save her."

Nathan's mind had been working overtime as they untied the ropes and released Leona.

"Anthony, you stay with Leona, I'll go after him and bring Fay back. Get Leona out of here now. She is bleeding and needs a medic. Send one of the others or come back yourself when she is safe."

Nathan knew that Leona felt she was deserting Fay but right now, in her emotional state, she was a hindrance rather than a help.

Anthony paused, but before he could argue, Nathan turned and started moving slowly forward.

"I'll send help as quick as I can Nathan" he whispered. "Don't take any risks." Anthony looked back as he spoke but couldn't see anything in the gloom and couldn't be sure Nathan had heard him. He seemed to have disappeared in the darkness.

Carefully Anthony lifted Leona to her knees. "Can you move," he asked.

She nodded. "I need to go back, Anthony. He is really on the edge there is no telling what he will do. From what I overheard they have met before. He is really intent on hurting Fay."

Anthony took her arm. "You have been injured. I'm not sure if that is mud or blood on your face and you can't stand. We need to get you out. Nathan will help Fay. I will send someone to help him." She nodded as he gently tugged her arm and slowly they made their way towards the entrance.

Chapter 25

Nathan knew that Anthony would send Chris or Jerry to assist him as soon as he could. By now someone would have gone to the cave where the smugglers were tied up to check on them. Hopefully they would realise further help was needed, someone might already be on their way.

He stopped and listened, but apart from his own breathing he could hear nothing. If only he knew how near he was, at least he would know when to hold back. The last thing he needed was to get too close and spook Thomas. People often act in the heat of the moment and Nathan was concerned that Thomas might just kill Fay if he was startled or felt threatened.

He had to handle this carefully. From what he had already seen, and from Leona's concerns, things were looking bad for Fay. He knew Thomas would not think twice about hurting her.

All kinds of thoughts on why she was here with Thomas were racing round in his head, and with an effort he ignored them. His job now was to stop Thomas escaping without Fay getting hurt.

He was still trying to think of way of doing this as he slowly crawled along the tunnel. The uneven floor, littered with rubble meant a silent approach was not an option. Cautiously, he kept inching forward hoping his approach would not give Thomas a reason to become violent and hurt Fay or start firing his gun blindly into the darkness of the tunnel. Right now, Thomas had the upper hand Nathan didn't want to help him gain a bigger advantage.

It felt like he was crawling for hours. In reality he knew it was only minutes, but still he heard no other noise. The tunnel seemed to be widening and veering to his left, and there was a cool breeze wafting round him, which was carrying the sound of voices with it. He stopped, hoping for sounds that would help him locate Thomas, and annoyed when all he could hear was the whistle of the wind and water drips in the tunnel.

Light was what he needed, but then that would help the gunman as well. There was a torch in his pocket, using it would light the tunnel a little but make him a sitting duck. He didn't intend to allow Thomas to use him as target practice. There was a definite change in the air current which momentarily confused him. He tried to work out what was causing this breeze.

He remembered Leona's comments about where Fay was being taken – something about her being tied up and a platform. Nathan tried to picture his recent visit to the tunnels in his mind. Left hand side of the tunnel, sticks out from the rock face. His next thought sent a chill through him. The viewing area hangs over a long drop to the rocks below.

The platform, of course that was what Leona said. He'd seen it on his visit to view the caves but had forgotten about it. That must be what she meant. Nathan had been trying to ignore his concern for Fay but this platform and the danger it presented to her increased his sense of urgency.

Stopping again he listened. Nothing except the odd sound of water drips and wind whistling; now he was sure he was near the opening for the viewing platform. He moved forward carefully, not wanting to startle Thomas, who still had the upper hand.

Edging forward inches at a time and stopping regularly to listen for voices or any kind of movement, Nathan was becoming more concerned. It had been some time since he'd heard anything. Just as he was about to move forward again he heard movement ahead. His eyes strained to see through the darkness, there it was again. His hand went to his pocket to pull out his torch. No! He left it where it was. If it is Thomas I might give him just the light he needs to shoot me.

This man is desperate, I can't give him any reason to use his gun. Right now I am Fay's only chance of leaving the cave alive.

Leaning against the cave wall Nathan waited, listening, hoping to get some idea of a direction and how close the sound was. After what seemed like an age he heard the noise again. The cave distorted the sound but it seemed someone was coming towards him, but occasionally stumbling, kicking against the tunnel walls. He just couldn't be sure from which direction.

Could it be Fay? Was she free and blundering her way through the darkness of the caves, falling as she tried to walk down the tunnel in the dark. That wouldn't make sense, Thomas letting her go just like that, she was his bargaining chip. If not Fay, could it be that help was not far behind him? If it was one of his colleagues he wished they would approach more carefully. He had no desire to alarm Thomas.

Slowly he began to edge forward again, pausing only to listen for sounds that would give him a clue as to how far he was from Thomas and Fay, or who was in the tunnel with them. His ears became ultra-sensitive, tuning into the slightest sound in the darkness. Even water dripping through the rocks onto the tunnel floor sounded like thunder.

There it was again the sound of bumping against the cave walls. He was sure he had heard movement this time. The sounds had come from behind him, not in front and Thomas could not have got round him. It had to be Anthony or one of the others. He decided to wait a for a few seconds to try and gauge how close they were.

Looking down the tunnel he thought he could make out a shadow. He had to be sure before he moved on. Waiting with his hand in his gun, he still wasn't sure who it was approaching. As the shadow got closer he continued to stare and then thought it could be Jerry. There was a faint glow as he approached. Then he heard someone whisper.

"Sorry it took so long I tripped over some rough ground back there. What's happening, have you found them?"

Nathan sighed in relief, realising it was Jerry. Shaking his head, he pointed into the gloom ahead, indicating that he thought they were somewhere in front of him. Jerry had a small torch in his hand and he instantly turned it off. He'd already heard shots and could see no point in giving the smuggler any help. They were in total darkness again; the only sounds being dripping water and the noise of a slight breeze.

Jerry realised that eventually he may have to risk using the torch. He crouched down by Nathan allowing his eyes time to start focusing. The he saw Nathan, his finger over his mouth to let Jerry know that silence was important, and he was indicating that the smuggler was still in the tunnel ahead of them. Jerry sat perfectly still, waiting for Nathan to lead the way.

They listened for a few seconds, there were no more noises. He looked at Jerry and pointed up the tunnel, then moved forward with Jerry close behind.

Thank goodness he had a torch, that meant together they could create some kind of light when they needed to. He was in no doubt Thomas had a lamp or some means of light, which was giving the flickering glimmer on the walls of the tunnel. It was one big advantage he had over them; that and having Fay as his hostage.

They edged forward until the breeze became much stronger. Jerry cautiously moved over to the opposite side of the tunnel, swearing silently as he moved some of the loose rubble. In the silence of the tunnel it sounded deafening. They both stopped, hoping the noise had not reached the other man. Then just as they were about to move forward again, Thomas shouted out.

"Go on come closer and I will drop her. I can hear you even though I may not be able to see you. Rest assured the minute I do she will go." His laugh echoed down the tunnel.

"Don't think I won't, I'm not going back inside for anyone, if she goes I go with her." His voice was shaky but he sounded as if he meant every word.

"Don't be daft man, what's a few years behind bars? Your life is worth more than that." Nathan responded. "Anyway, if you hurt her and by some miracle live, you'll be locked up for life. Give up now before anyone else gets hurt."

There was silence.

Then just as Nathan was going to call out again Fay cried out as if in pain.

"He's got me tied to the platform he said he is going to kill us both if you don't back off."

Her voice was shrill and shaky. "He wants you to let him walk out with me, if you don't he will carry out his threat." Her voice broke as she said the last words, the sound of sobbing reached Jerry and Nathan.

"We can't do that, you know we can't." Nathan waited for Thomas to respond. Then they heard Fay speaking to Thomas.

'Good girl, Jerry thought, keep him occupied and give us a chance to get nearer.' He looked over to Nathan and signalled they should move now. They were both still trying to listen to the conversation between Fay and her kidnapper. Nathan signalled they should wait a bit longer.

"Why are you doing this to me? What did I do to make you hate me so much? It was you who betrayed me, Thomas, I loved you."

He laughed. "I'll tell you why. If you hadn't been so pure and innocent, then I wouldn't have gone to jail. I was looking for a bit of fun, you were so naïve, easy to fool, then I discovered you were loaded so I decided to get my hands on your money. A bit of sport along the way was an added bonus and I would have enjoyed teaching you how to treat a man."

Fay shook her head. "I don't understand Thomas, I loved you and believed you loved me."

He laughed again. "Loved you? Don't be stupid. I prefer my women with a bit more experience. Your money is what I loved." He laughed at Fay's gasp on hearing his words.

"When Debra found out about you, she wasn't happy to just ruin my plans, she wanted revenge. She went to the police, told them about one or two of my less than legal deals. The police did some digging and found out I was already married."

Fay interrupted him, "Already married. You never loved me! Why is this my fault, it was me who got hurt. I loved you."

Thomas suddenly seemed to lose control and slapped Fay making here head spin. He grabbed her arms and she cried out in pain and fear.

"Oh little miss innocent. If you had married me I would have had fun with you for a couple of months then left you, taking your money with me. Debra would have been happy helping me spend it. None of this would have happened." His voice was so full of hatred she was afraid to speak

"Oh no! You held out on me and spoilt my plans. Then when I saw you at the casino I thought I was going to get my revenge at last. Just when I thought it was payback time your hero burst in, spoiling my fun." He continued to hold on to her, bruising her arms and shaking her.

"Now you have fouled up this job. It isn't wise to mess with the men behind this, there will be a price to pay and I am not going to pay it. You owe me big time Fay, and this time the price is my life or yours." He loosened his hold.

"Love you, you must be joking. It takes more of a woman than you to get my love. Your money on the other hand, I loved the thought of spending that." He moved closer as he spat the words out and Fay felt spittle hit her face.

She couldn't speak. Just sat in silence staring at this man who she had loved and believed loved her. How could she have been so easily duped.

Then he spoke again, still within inches of her face.

"Yes, it is payback time. The price is your life Fay. Unless I am allowed to walk free, you and I will live together in eternity, just as you dreamed of many years ago." Thomas laughed, enjoying his joke and the look of fear on her face.

She felt a tremor run through her, sobbing as tears began running down her cheeks, she tried to find the strength to accept the situation she was in. Thomas hated her so completely she was in no doubt that he would kill her if his demands weren't met. A feeling of resignation began to creep over her as she waited for him to make the next move.

'Today is the day I die' she thought.

Chapter 26

Nathan felt anger, fear and frustration run through him as he heard this exchange. His instinct was to rush forward and rescue Fay, his training told him otherwise.

Somewhere deep inside he realised he cared for Fay, he was experiencing similar feelings to those he'd had when Lou died, but this time he could do something about it. This time he could save the woman he now realised he was falling in love with.

Pulling back, he pressed himself against the wall and looked across at Jerry.

"I am going to stay here and tell him that we agree, you pretend to go back make enough noise so that he believes you have gone," he whispered. "When he moves forward I will be waiting."

Jerry nodded, "I won't be too far away." He started to go back through the tunnel and heard Nathan calling out to Thomas.

"OK, we want your hostage to leave here unharmed, so we have no alternative but to agree to your demands. I want to see her first to make sure she is unhurt. It's just me now the others have gone back to give us space."

There was silence then Thomas's voice rang out echoing round the cave walls.

"OK, just remember make one wrong move and we both go. Come forward with your arms in the air. If I see anyone else or any weapons I will jump. Remember we are tied together."

His voice was too calm, the calm before a storm. Nathan knew that Thomas was on the edge and in danger of losing control. He stood up slowly, wary in case Thomas took a shot at him.

Walking forward with his gun tucked in the back of his waistband, he held his arms high hoping Thomas would believe him to be unarmed.

He was careful to approach slowly and as he rounded a twist in the tunnel two shadows came into sight. The lamp Thomas was holding swayed in the breeze, momentarily dazzling Nathan, his eyes not used to so much light. They slowly adjusted, enabling him to take stock of the situation.

Thomas was holding Fay by a rope tied around her neck. He could see even in the dim light that she was on the edge of a platform. If she went, Thomas would go with her and vice versa. Whilst he was assessing the situation he heard muffled sounds behind him.

It sounded as if back up was on the way. Hopefully it was Jerry returning, and right now he needed all the help he could get. Turning his attention back to Thomas and Fay he called out.

"I can't see her in this light I'm going to reach into my pocket for my torch." He could see Fay in the light from Thomas's lamp, although not clearly, but was playing for time hoping assistance was close by.

"No you don't! Try it and I will kill her." Thomas shouted his voice now was shaky. He tugged at the rope making Fay cry out.

"Look be reasonable, I can't negotiate with you until I have seen she is OK."

Nathan waited hoping he would agree to him using his torch.

"OK, but if you hope to pull a gun on me be warned I will shoot her before you have time to get a shot in."

"OK." Nathan pulled out a small torch and flicked it on and off to let Thomas know it wasn't a gun.

It created a small glimmer of light in the tunnel which didn't help him see Fay any clearer, but hopefully Thomas would not realise this was a ploy. He was thinking on his feet, trying to find ways to create a delay till help came.

"What do you hope to gain by this? Even if you get out there will always be someone after you. Let her go."

He tried to get a better look at Fay. Her head was at an awkward angle so he couldn't see her clearly enough but knew she must be terrified and only just about holding on.

"I won't let her go until I am well away. I have sea passage and friends to help me so don't waste your breath trying to persuade me otherwise." Thomas saw Nathan move. "And don't come any closer. I don't have much to live for and she owes me." He pushed Fay then tugged at the rope causing her to cry out again.

"Oh! Now I know who you are. The hero of the hour. I knew you voice was familiar. So Fay, you are not so innocent as I thought." Thomas sneered as he recognized Nathan.

"Well if we go off the platform that will be two scores settled, won't it." Thomas laughed, enjoying his joke.

Nathan knew that Thomas would be even less inclined to negotiate now he had recognized him. He had no alternative but to back off, he'd be putting Fay at risk if he didn't. Tackling Thomas was out of the question, if he failed then Fay would almost certainly die.

"OK, so we have met before, it doesn't change anything. The platform, it's not safe, I don't want any unintentional accidents. Just move onto safer ground."

Thomas seemed to think about this and then turned slightly and edged forward pulling Fay with him. Nathan moved backwards down the tunnel putting a little more space between them hoping that they would follow him and walk further away from the platform. Then the rope seemed to tighten so they couldn't move from the platform, Fay fell to floor crying out as the rope squeezed against her throat.

"Sorry, no can do, guess we are at the end of the rope." He laughed at his sick joke, as he shouted back to Nathan.

Nathan thought again about rushing Thomas but knew that Fay would get hurt and anyway he was sure that backup was close, he could sense someone was hiding in the gloom. 'I only hope I am right', he thought. He had to stop Thomas from realising he had help otherwise he might decide to take his own life and Fay's as he had threatened.

Nathan watched as Fay struggled to get to her feet but before she could stand she was pushed back to her knees. Then he realised Thomas was looking towards him. He seemed to look over Nathan's shoulder into the gloom as if he could see something there. Hesitating for a second he didn't move then he smiled and looked as if he was about to speak, but before he could utter a sound the look on his face seemed to change to one of shocked surprise.

Without warning a shot rang out behind Nathan, the bullet whizzed past his head barely missing him and hit Thomas.

Thomas's body jerked back as the bullet hit him. He fell backwards crashing onto the platform, his weight shook the platform as he fell to the floor, his body rolling over the edge dragging Fay with him.

Nathan leapt forward and reached out just managing to grab her ankle.

He could feel the man's weight pulling them all backwards to the edge of the platform, then he heard Fay choking as the rope tightened.

Desperately holding onto her with one hand he searched his pocket and pulled out a knife.

His grip was beginning to loosen with the weight of their bodies hanging on the rope. He slid his free hand up Fay's side until he could feel the rope. Putting his arm round her shoulder he used the rope to pull himself further onto the platform; praying it would hold his weight and that he wouldn't hurt Fay. She was struggling trying to free herself, the rope tightened and she started gasping for breath.

He felt her going limp as he tried cutting the rope with the knife. Damn, it was useless. Frustration and fear coursed through him. He tugged at the rope where it was tied to the rail trying to slacken it so that Fay could breath.

Suddenly without warning the rope snapped. Thomas's body weight and his hacking with the knife must have caused it to weaken.

Without the weight of Thomas's body the rope loosened a little and they both rolled to one side. He could feel the platform shuddering under the sudden movement. Reaching out he grabbed Fay's arm. Then he felt someone tugging at his legs pulling them both back off the platform to safety.

"Hold on Nathan, I've got you, keep hold of her." Chris shouted as he struggled to pull them back to solid ground.

"Is she OK?" Chris asked. "What happened, did he fall?"

"Yes, no thanks to you. You stupid bastard, why did you shoot him? I was getting through to him." Nathan shouted at Chris. "You nearly got us all killed." His voice was filled with rage. It was only his concern for Fay that stopped him punching Chris.

Bending over Fay, who was unconscious but no longer choking, he checked her breathing. Nathan saw the bruising around her neck and felt anger at the thought of what could have happened.

"Lucky for you, Chris she's breathing." He cut through the remaining strands of the rope. "I need some light here, give me your torch."

"Sorry I didn't realise I thought he was going to jump." Chris said. Nathan again resisted the temptation to take a swing at Chris and continued to help Fay.

Just then Emma appeared with a light closely followed by Jerry and Luchiano.

"Are you OK? We heard a gunshot." Looking around to see if any one was hurt Emma saw Fay. "Oh no, please tell me she is OK!"

Nathan nodded. "Unfortunately Thomas isn't. Better get it confirmed, but he went off the platform and if the bullet didn't kill him the fall probably has."

"Who fired the shot?" Luchiano asked.

Before Nathan could say anything, Chris spoke. "I did. I thought he was going to jump and take the girl with him."

"OK. Well we'll sort all that out later, let's get the young lady back to the medics." As Luchiano spoke Fay began to murmur.

Nathan bent over her but Emma waved him away. "I'll come back with her. You go on with Chris and Jerry. Luchiano, will you stay and help us?" Nathan hesitated, she put her hand on his shoulder and gently pushed him away. "Go on, the others need your help. We can manage until the medics arrive."

Jerry walked up behind Nathan and whispered. "Something is fishy about all this. When I went back down the tunnel I waited until I thought it was safe then started walking back to you. Someone jumped me, knocked me out. Emma and Luchiano found me as I was coming round."

Jerry fell in behind Chris as they went to get help, glancing quickly in Nathan's direction. Nathan nodded in acknowledgement of Jerry's comment, looked back at Fay and reluctantly walked down the tunnel.

Something certainly didn't add up. He started going over what had just happened. There shouldn't have been anyone else behind Jerry unless it was one of their people. Why had Chris shot Thomas? He could have given them valuable information. Did Thomas smile, as Nathan had thought? Did he know Chris, if so he'd not been afraid of him, from his expression he was pleased to see him.

As he worked through his doubts his suspicions began to have a ring of truth in them. If I am right, then we have found the source of the leaks.

Emma tried to calm Fay as they slowly made their way back to the cave entrance.

"Leona is fine and more worried about you than herself. Now stop trying to talk, you are safe now. By now the medics will have taken her down to the inlet where she can be checked over."

Luchiano was almost carrying her as she was still struggling to breathe and her legs and arms were stiff from being in one position for so long.

"Try not to think about what happened. We can talk it out later, you just focus on the fact you are free." He tried to encourage her. "Besides it's not doing your throat any good talking, everything can wait until you are feeling better."

Progress was horribly slow but in the distance they could see light coming into the tunnel and heard people moving about. Hopefully the medics were on their way. Emma had some water with her and she sprinkled some on Fay's face but wouldn't let her drink it, she couldn't risk Fay choking. She was so angry with herself, that she had not made more of an effort to check on Fay, especially when no one heard from either her or Leona.

The flickering lights were closer and they could see faint shadows moving their way, help was nearer. Emma suggested they sit and wait for the medics rather than walk Fay any further. Shock was beginning to set in and Fay was silently crying and shaking from head to toe.

As they waited, Emma was thinking about what had happened. Something was wrong. Why had Chris shot that man? The usual procedure was to take people into custody whenever possible, in the hope of gaining information. Who knocked Jerry out? The only people behind him were police or customs. Anthony had appeared with Leona from the tunnel. What the heck were they doing there? She looked across at Luchiano and could see he was deep in thought.

'I can't wait for the debrief,' she thought.

The medics finally arrived and suddenly everything seemed to be happening. Emma said she would stay with them and help Fay.

Inspector Luchiano decided to get back to the others to ensure that everything was under control. He had a lot on his mind and the sooner he got answers the better.

When Jerry, Chris and Nathan appeared at the tunnel mouth, Nathan could see that Anthony was watching over five men, presumably those caught in the caves and one caught down on the beach whilst trying to make their escape in the small boat.

Anthony nodded, acknowledging the three men. He thought that Nathan looked agitated, but he avoided getting into conversation.

Jerry walked over to help watch over the smugglers.

"Is Leona OK?"

"Yes, she's in the ambulance just waiting for Fay to arrive. She won't go without her, it seems.

"Fay is OK isn't she?" Jerry asked. "I understand there was gunfire."

Nathan joined them. "There was. The medics should be bringing Fay out soon. It was a close call though. The other man was shot and went off the platform whilst Fay was still tied to him."

He wanted to avoid any more questions. The priority was keeping an eye on Chris and the prisoners to see if there were any signs of recognition between them. He sat down next to Chris. Later, when the girls were safe, he would think this out but right now he needed to focus on their safety.

Much later, back at the hotel, Nathan went over what had happened. The operation had been successful, they had got the drugs, a small amount of arms, and the smugglers were in custody. Both the girls were safe and receiving medical care in the local hospital.

He knew that once the prisoners realised the length of sentences they were facing, one of them would start talking, giving information on the ring leaders in the hope of cutting a deal.

There was rarely honour amongst thieves.

Chapter 27

Chris however was another matter. If it was proved he was the source of the leak then he could look forward to a long sentence and a hard time in prison. He would be guilty of smuggling and assisting in kidnap and the murder of Thomas, all of which would bring a heavy sentence.

Betraying his colleagues placed him in no man's land. He would be shunned by them and his fellow prisoners who would enjoy paying him back for their own grievances against the customs. He might even be inside with men he had helped put away, and they would make his life hell.

Nathan thought that right now Chris would be trying to work out a convincing reason for killing Thomas. Somehow Nathan didn't think he would persuade anyone to believe him. Hopefully Luchiano was right and he wouldn't run.

Nathan and Inspector Luchiano had spoken briefly and decided to let Chris think he was home free and the hero of the hour. He was being watched and would be arrested for questioning after the debriefing in the morning or before if he decided his cover was blown and made a run for it. One thing for sure, he was going to be in prison a long time if he was guilty.

Fay and Leona were kept in hospital overnight for observation. Fay was to be checked out by a throat specialist, to make sure she would not have any lasting problems. Leona was relatively unscathed, with just one cut where Thomas had hit her, and some bruising and rope burns. Leona and Fay refused to be separated, it was as if their ordeal had forged a bond between them.

Nathan sat on his bed, his mind refusing to rest. Now that everything was over he had to admit his feelings for Fay were stronger than he had dared to imagine. When he thought she was in danger it brought back the empty, helpless feeling he'd had when Lou and Duncan died.

He was not sure he could deal with loving someone again, and having to risk the pain of loss a second time. He also knew that walking away from Fay would not be any easier. Turning out the light he lay down, eventually falling into a restless sleep, woken only by the alarm at 6.30am.

Chapter 28

Inspector Luchiano was in the office early, he needed to read all the reports and check everything that had taken place and work out his course of action. He had talked long into the night with his team and it appeared clear that Chris Trun was the probable source of the leaks. This situation demanded careful handling. They had to be sure there was enough evidence to get a conviction, he thought there was enough evidence to present to customs.

The informant who had been working with Luchiano's team was a resident of the island. He had been in contact from the yacht the dealers were using and confirmed that he was certain that Chris was the person leaking information to the gang. Working undercover as one of the crew, he was in the best place to find evidence to confirm their suspicions and to make sure the yacht owner and crew were arrested as well.

This man had lost his son to drugs and had worked undercover for Luchiano since his son's death. He'd volunteered to remain on board till the yacht docked and was boarded by customs. Brave man, the Inspector thought, if his cover was broken he would surely be killed, his body probably never found.

His mind returned to Chris. He had been liked by everyone and considered to be a decent guy. Luchiano had known him some time and worked with him on many joint operations. Now he had endangered the life of both police and customs officers and one of his oldest friends.

A promising career thrown away for what, money, pure greed? Well, whatever his reasons they would do him no good where he was going.

The evidence they had been gathering along with the latest events and the fresh information from their informant left little room for doubt. Apparently Chris had made friends with the wrong people. Possibly they lured him in on something small and then, when he was in too deep, sprung this job on him.

Already one of the smugglers had started talking in the hope of getting a lighter sentence; apparently he didn't want to be charged as an accessory to murder. That, added to kidnap and smuggling meant he would be sent down for a long time.

According to the prisoner, Chris had been hiding the drugs on the island, awaiting instructions. He'd also helped hide one of the gang in the caves. The drugs were to be repacked into small boxes in the caves ready for shipping, then taken down to the nearby cove. There they would be loaded onto the small boat during the night, ready to be transferred to a yacht.

The signal would be sent to the yacht when the boat was loaded and ready to transfer its cargo. The yacht would then sail close to shore to meet the boat and transfer the drugs. By sailing under cover of darkness and with Chris helping them, they planned to be well away by morning.

With this testimony, Luchiano had confirmation that his suspicions regarding Chris were right, he was obviously leaking information. He had probably informed the smugglers of Nathan's arrival, which answered the question as to why they had moved sooner than expected. If the case was solid and the court found him guilty he was now facing a charge of murder and accessory to kidnap.

He probably thought he'd got away with it. Luchiano's men were watching him to make sure he didn't disappear before all the evidence could be consolidated, then he would be arrested and charged.

Chris had been told to report for debriefing later than everyone else, Luchiano didn't want any more unpleasantness with other people Chris had deceived or put into danger within the department. The police and customs worked together on the island, and he knew his team would be pretty angry when they found out Chris had been the source of the leaks.

He decided he would read the reports again, checking every detail. He didn't want the case thrown out of court on a technicality. An hour after he had started reading through all the information his secretary arrived and made him coffee. As he looked up, she smiled.

"Another bad day at the office?

"Here are the files for the meeting. Oh, I stopped off and bought you a pastry; didn't think you would have had time for breakfast."

Luchiano smiled. Dee had been his secretary for so long she knew him almost as well as his wife. He drank his coffee and as he ate his makeshift breakfast the thought crossed his mind that perhaps it was time to take a back seat and spend more time with his family. The bang of the outer door focused his mind on the debrief, the fleeting thought of retirement forgotten.

Emma and Anthony arrived first closely followed by Jerry. Emma pounced immediately she walked into the office.

"You, Luchiano, are in my bad books. You knew all along about Anthony's career choice and never gave me a hint, knowing how I would feel about him being in that line of work. Or about my alleged future daughter-in-law. I thought we were friends."

He smiled. "For the same reason I didn't tell him you worked for me." He pulled a chair out for Emma.

Nathan had entered the room in time to hear the exchange and smiled. "If it's any consolation Emma, you weren't the only one in the dark."

He sat down nodding at the others in the room. "What is the plan of action then?" he addressed his remark to Inspector Luchiano.

"Well you all know that Chris is the main suspect regarding the leaking of information. He will be coming in after this debrief. I would appreciate it if you try to avoid him. He will be arrested after you have all left the building. I have given him some leeway to hand himself in, but I think he will try to bluff it out. We now have enough evidence to charge him, but he is unaware of that." He sighed, stood up and perched on the corner of his desk.

"Early this morning one of the smugglers started spilling the beans. We know enough to build a picture of exactly what has been going on. I'm just glad the feeling of mistrust will be gone from my station." He paused allowing his words to sink in.

"Shame, when I first knew Chris he was a great guy with a good future in front of him." Luchiano picked up some papers and shuffled them into a neat pile then sat down behind his desk.

"Anyway, I have read all your reports. I just need to tie up some loose ends up in the paperwork. Then you can all get some rest." Luchiano hesitated. He knew how difficult this was for everyone, they all felt betrayed. Customs and police worked side by side and there was an unspoken understanding of trust. Chris's betrayal had damaged that trust.

"Well, first I want to say well done everyone. We found a substantial haul of drugs and some guns in the cave, and the yacht is now under surveillance by the coast guards. We hope it will go back to its base then we can move in and make some more arrests."

He looked around the room; everyone was looking serious and avoiding eye contact with their colleagues. "I have spoken to the hospital and it seems the two young ladies have not sustained any serious injuries, and I have confirmation that their attacker was found to be dead when they got to him."

The room remained silent, everyone seemed lost in their own thoughts. Often the euphoria of a successful operation was followed by thoughts of what could have been.

"That pretty much clears things up so when you have finished your paperwork I suggest you all take a few hours off. I already have Leona's report so the sooner the rest of you get yours completed the better."

Jerry was the first to move. He spoke briefly to Nathan, letting him know he had passed him the notes at the hotel. Then saying a general goodbye, he left the room, the others followed him almost immediately.

The customs would be going through a similar meeting and their men who would be feeling the same sense of anger and disbelief. Betrayal by a fellow officer or comrade was hard to accept, and none of them would feel like celebrating this particular arrest.

Luchiano looked at the pile of papers on his desk and started going through his in tray, finding it hard to concentrate. If only he could take a few days off, his family wouldn't recognise him soon. His office door opened and Emma appeared.

"I don't expect you are going to get a rest, but if you fancy a coffee or something stronger give me a call." She knew how difficult it was going to be for him to arrest Chris.

Luchiano smiled. "Actually Emma, I was going to call you." He looked at his watch, yes he had a few minutes. "Now is as good a time as any." He pointed to a chair, she walked over and sat down wondering what was coming.

Luchiano didn't know of an easy way to say what he had to say, so he came straight out with it.

"Emma, I believe we may have found out who killed Frank and Angel." He paused, waiting for his words to sink in. They had become friends over the years and he hated causing Emma's pain to resurface.

"If things go according to plan and the information is sound, there will be an arrest fairly soon." Emma sat perfectly still.

"I promise you we will do everything to nail them and if it is in my power they will stand trial." Luchiano watched as Emma's face turned white, tears slowly made tracks across her cheeks. He waited for her to speak.

She had a thousand questions but couldn't get any of them out, until after what seemed an eternity, she simply nodded, stood up and left the office, not knowing what to feel after all these years. She didn't even notice the tears silently rolling down her face or the strange look the secretary gave her as she walked past her desk.

Luchiano sat for a few moments gathering his own thoughts. Then he buzzed his secretary. "Chris Trun will be here shortly. When you have shown him in, go for a coffee, things could get a bit nasty, it would be better if you weren't here. I would like to handle this without too much fuss." He looked at the clock and sat back to wait for Chris.

Chapter 29

Fay and Leona were out of hospital and enjoying being mothered by Emma. She had insisted Fay stay with her so she could keep an eye on her. Fay sensed somehow that there was another reason why Emma wanted her to stay, but she couldn't work out what it was. Emma was never one to talk about her inner feelings.

Nathan had been a constant visitor and whilst he said little to the others he had talked in depth to Fay. He told her about his family and she had told him about hers and her relationship with Thomas.

They had each talked about their past lives and agreed that their relationship should be taken slowly to allow them both time to come to terms with the past, and to be sure of how strong their feelings for each other were.

Fay confided in Emma, telling her that she knew already she was in love with Nathan and she was prepared to wait for him until he was ready start a new life with her.

Emma remembered how Frank had been cautious when they first met. He said later that he couldn't believe someone as wonderful as her could love him. Emma smiled, she had seen the way Nathan looked at Fay and could not have been happier. She knew that there would be many problems, Nathan's line of work being the biggest, but she also knew that Fay loved him, heart and soul, and together they would overcome any problem that arose.

Nathan had been working for the police on the mainland and had been asked to go undercover on this operation as he was unknown to anyone on the island. It appeared he had not known of Anthony's career either.

Anthony and Leona were the big surprise. He worked for Customs and had been brought in to work on the current case because of his knowledge of the island. It had been hoped he would be able to use his contacts to help in finding the source of the leaks in the department.

Leona was not his fiancé, but was an operative who Anthony had worked with before. This made the cover story of a wedding easier to be more convincing. Leona had then been asked to check out Fay, who had for a short time been a suspect, mainly because of her connection with Thomas.

After her initial surprise, Emma accepted that although this was not the line of work she had wanted for her son, it was his chosen career. Also it seemed that he and Leona had formed a genuine relationship during the operation. She liked Leona and was hoping the relationship would blossom.

I suppose something good has come out of all this, Emma smiled to herself, thinking of the two couples who were so important in her life. If these youngsters have found love in the midst of such danger then something positive had come out of all this.

The news that Luchiano had given her came briefly into her head. Instantly she pushed it away, not yet ready to face it. That was one of the reasons she had asked Fay to stay with her; having someone to fuss over kept her from thinking.

If Nathan and Fay did marry, where would they live, she thought. Losing Fay would be like losing a daughter. Her mind suddenly went in all directions. If they were to marry where would their wedding be? I hope it would be here in Gibraltar and I get to see my 'daughter' married. Maybe one day Leona and Anthony will marry and return to live here. She let her mind wander, imagining her life surrounded by the people she loved most in the world.

Suddenly warm tears were trickling down her cheeks, as she remembered the pain of losing her beloved husband and daughter. Trying hard to fight back tears she continued thinking of the possibilities for both couples. One or both couples could have children and she would be a grandmother. Maybe a little girl like my Angel and a boy named Frank. Tears trickled across her cheeks, unchecked they splashed on the photograph she held.

If Frank was here he would say 'Come on old girl, you're getting a bit carried away.' Emma smiled. Frank would have been so proud of Anthony and he would have loved Fay. She would have been taken under his wing. He always wanted to nurture people who he felt were floundering in this world.

She sighed and looked at the photograph of her husband and baby, then as she so often did, silently spoke to them.

'With the imminent arrest of your murderers and the possibility of these four wonderful people finding love, then could it be that finally, Frank my dear, my life could be almost complete? Might I, after all these years, find some peace to ease the pain of losing you and our darling Angel? I so want to stop being angry with you both for leaving me.'

She sat for a while, quietly allowing her mind to fill with hopes and dreams of the future, visualising her life with the people she most loved around her. As her mind rambled on, Emma heard someone whisper very close to her ear.

'At last my love, at last.'

She didn't need to look round. She knew who had spoken, but if she looked there would be no one there.

She knew that voice so very well, and heard it often in her sleep. It was Frank's voice she heard.

* * * * * * *